Zhang Shouchen and Others

Traditional
Comic Tales

Translated by Gladys Yang

Panda Books

Panda Books
First Edition 1983
Reprinted 1990
Copyright 1983 by CHINESE LITERATURE PRESS
ISBN 0-8351-1165-2
ISBN 7-5071-0063-4/I.57

Published by CHINESE LITERATURE PRESS, Beijing (37), China
Distributed by China International Book Trading Corporation
21 Chegongzhuang Xilu, Beijing 100044, China
P.O. Box 399, Beijing, China
Printed in the People's Republic of China

CONTENTS

Preface

THESE comic tales are a form of *xiangsheng* (pronounced "she-ang sheng"), literally "face and voice", the satirical, laughter-evoking performing art with the largest audience in China. *Xiangsheng* artists can dispense with a stage or stage props, but they must be good singers, elocutionists, comedians and mimics. There are usually two performers. However, the stories presented here are "single-mouth *xiangsheng*" — solos.

It is claimed by some that the ancestors of *xiangsheng* were the court jesters of old who told stories or cracked jokes to amuse their masters. But *xiangsheng* are not designed to entertain the aristocracy; like music-hall they are for the man in the street. The skills required for them were being perfected between the 11th and 13th centuries when populous mercantile cities grew up in south China with a host of merchants, small tradesmen, artisans and apprentices, all avid for amusement. By the end of the 13th century Hangzhou, the capital of Southern Song, had over one million inhabitants. Marco Polo described it as "the greatest city which may be found in the world, where so many pleasures may be found that one fancies himself to be in Paradise". To cater to the urban lower class, story-tellers, ballad-singers and many other folk artists performed daily in the streets, parks and tea-houses. To compete with rival showmen and capture an audience they had to be virtuosos. The story-tellers usually specialized in different subject matter: ghost stories, romances, tales of shrewd and upright judges, or Buddhist legends.... Moreover these stories were distinguished by their humour, their delight in puns and playing upon words, their mockery without malice, all of which are features of our modern *xiangsheng*. There were no *xiangsheng* then. But popular entertainers practised their arts through all the vicissitudes of Chinese history. And centuries later *xiangsheng* were able to draw on these earlier performing skills and some of the traditional repertory.

Xiangsheng took shape in the second half of the 19th century, in such north China cities as Baoding, Beijing and Tianjin where, significantly, *pingju* opera also evolved to satisfy those townsfolk who found it easier to appreciate than Peking Opera. One pioneer in this art form, Zhu Shaowen, trained first as a clown in Peking Opera. To start with, *xiangsheng* artists played in streets or market-places, some concealing themselves behind curtains to mimic the sounds of animals, children crying, a house on fire.... They then came into the open to crack jokes and perform *xiangsheng* drawn from traditional plays, tales and ballads, or based on topical events. In their efforts to raise a laugh they included not a few bawdy jokes — in those days their audiences were restricted to men. Their social status was low. They had no security, and to make a living often performed in brothels. Most illiterate apprentices learned their craft by imitating their masters' performances.

A *xiangsheng* artist of the second generation, Li Deyang, refined on the art form and gained such popularity that he was given the nickname "Everyone's Idol".

Thanks to his influence and that of his confrères, *xiang-sheng* now moved from the streets into theatres.

An outstanding comedian of the third generation was Zhang Shouchen (1898-1970), who compiled this collection of stories. A native of Beijing, at fifteen he was apprenticed to the *xiangsheng* performer Jiao Dehai, and he collaborated with "Everyone's Idol". He appreciated the artistic skills of the best traditional *xiangsheng* and opposed the vulgarity of certain items, which he edited and improved, although our readers are likely to find the humour in some of his stories rather crude. Well-known in Beijing, Tianjin, Jinan and Nanjing, he performed in duologue, solo and trio *xiangsheng*, creating original stories of his own to satirize the old society. After Liberation he concentrated on performing solo *xiangsheng*, training young artists, and compiling a collection of comic stories. Here we present only a selection of them, as the puns in many others defy translation.

As Zhang's stories evolved in the cities of north China in a semi-feudal context, most of them reflect the ideas of the urban lower class. They ridicule and expose the corruption, miserliness and ineptitude of old-time officials and landlords, the hypocrisy of feudal ethics, the foibles and strange adventures of small townsfolk and artisans. Akin to yet different from standard jokes and short stories, they have better characterization and fuller plots than the former and are more humorous than the latter, their jokes being an integral part of the recital, designed to bring out the main theme and reveal contradictions. The different incidents form a logical sequence without undue elaboration, and much is left to the listeners' imagination including, often, the conclusion and moral. For all their exaggeration they present a vivid and basically truthful picture of those bygone days. Some of them remind us of a Chaplin film in which the underdog, in spite of his quirks and apparent stupidity, gets a rise out of those with high position and power.

Since Liberation a host of new *xiangsheng* artists, both professional and amateur, has emerged. They received encouragement and help from such scholars as Luo Zhangpei and Wu Xiaoling, and the great writer Lao She who himself wrote *xiangsheng*. No other art form can compete with *xiangsheng* in the speed with which they reflect new topical issues. And the artists' social status is vastly improved; for as their performances go on the air to all parts of the country, helping to popularize the standard Beijing dialect, many of them are national celebrities — "Everyone's Idols".

Gladys Yang

Three Promotions in Succession

THE story I am going to tell today happened in the Ming Dynasty. In Linqing County, Shandong Province, there once lived a rich landlord and his family. The young master, Zhang Haogu, had been pampered ever since childhood and had never gone to school. After he grew up, he just idled away his time pleasure-seeking and doing all sorts of useless things. After having eaten and drunk his fill each day, he would saunter along the streets, carrying a bird cage, and people nicknamed him "puppy".

One day, as he was idling along the street, he saw a fortune-teller surrounded by a crowd. He decided to go up and take a look. No sooner had he edged himself into the crowd than the fortune-teller recognized him as "puppy" and wanted to get some money out of him by flattering him. Feigning interest he approached him and said, "Old brother, you have a pair of bright piercing eyes and heavy arched brows. You will turn out to be a great statesman. Your forehead is very high and broad, you have the makings of a high official. If you go to sit the imperial examination in Beijing, I'm sure you will pass it. I'll congratulate you then."

If Zhang Haogu had been a sensible person, he would have boxed the fortune-teller's ears when he heard this flattery. Since he couldn't even read or write his own name, how could he go to sit an examination in Beijing?

But he never thought of that! All he thought was: My family have plenty of money and it's easy for me to make my way to officialdom. Instead of getting angry, he felt rather pleased and said, "Are you sure I can pass the examination?"

"No question of it. You'll surely be one of the top three in the exam."

"Well, I'll give you two taels of silver now. If I really pass the examination, I'll give you more when I get back. If I don't, I'll settle accounts with you!" The fortune-teller thought to himself: I'll be long gone by then.

Back home, Zhang Haogu packed his luggage, took some gold and silver with him and left for Beijing. The question never crossed his mind as to just how an illiterate like him could sit an imperial exam in Beijing. Still, in the old society it happened!

By the time he reached Beijing it was the last day of the examination. The door of the West Gate had already been closed, but as luck would have it, he happened to meet a team of water-carts going into the city. During the Ming and Qing Dynasties the emperors liked to drink spring water from Jade Spring Mountain in the Beijing suburbs and fresh water had to be delivered to the city nightly. Zhang Haogu, not knowing this, rode through the gate behind the team of water-carts. The guards, thinking he was an escort from the imperial palace, let him pass.

Once inside the city, he didn't know where to look for the examination hall. He just rode willy-nilly along the streets. When he came to a crossroad, he saw a group of people carrying two lanterns approaching. In the middle of the crowd was an official — Prince Wei

Zhongxian on night patrol. This frightened Zhang Haogu's horse which stampeded. Zhang tried to rein it in but failed and the horse ran into Wei's. In the past Wei would have killed him at once, since he was the favourite eunuch of Emperor Xizong and had the power to execute anyone before reporting to the emperor. But today he wanted to know first who this person was. So he reined in his horse and shouted, "Are you tired of living, fellow?" Not knowing he was Prince Wei, the young "puppy" shouted back, "Don't talk to me like that. I have something urgent to do!" "What is it?" "I've hurried all the way from Shandong to sit the imperial examination. If I'm late, I won't be among the top three." "Are you sure you'll be one of the top three?" "If not, I wouldn't have come here." "But the examination hall has closed now and you can't get in." "I can knock at the gate."

Wei thought to himself: He said he would be one of the top three. Is he really that qualified? He's just boasting, and putting me off with big words! So he shouted, "All right! Give him my card and let him be admitted to the examination hall!" Wei was curious to find out whether or not the man was really qualified.

In the end, of course, Wei was an idiot. If he'd wanted to know how good Zhang was, it would have been enough to allow him in. But why give him his personal card? Card in hand, Zhang was deliriously happy, and was even given a guide to lead him to the examination hall.

Upon arriving, they knocked at the gate and handed in the card. Seeing that it was Prince Wei's, the two chief examiners promptly jumped up. One said, "This man is sent by Prince Wei, he must be a relative of his.

We must admit him." "No," countered the other, "all our rooms are filled." "Well, we ought to do what we can to make room for him. He must be Prince Wei's relative. Otherwise, why would he be here at this time of night? We'll have to quickly vacate a room for him. We must do so even if the two of us have to stay outside all night." "Then, we'd better . . . stay outside." Saying this, they invited Zhang in. Having thought for a while, the two examiners tried to decide what to do.

One said, "Let's give him the paper."

"No," said the other, "we don't even know which books he's reviewed. If the subjects aren't suitable and he can't answer the questions correctly and fails, we'll offend the prince." "What shall we do then?" "Well, here are the examination papers. We'll do them for him. I'll give the answer and you write it down."

So they completed the paper for him. Then they thought: "If we give him No. 1 that will be a little too obvious. All right, let him come second."

So without writing a word Zhang Haogu came in second.

Two days later, all the successful candidates went to pay their respects to the chief examiners. But Zhang Haogu did not. After all he didn't know any of the protocol.

The two examiners became puzzled again. One said, "Zhang Haogu doesn't seem to know the rules. Although he was sent by Prince Wei, he would never have been No. 2 if we hadn't helped. He's a little too unreasonable, not even coming to thank us!" "Never mind. We're only doing it for Prince Wei's sake. He sent Zhang here with his own card at midnight. Zhang must be a relative or a close friend.   When he becomes a high official, we'll need him to look after us.   It doesn't matter if he doesn't come to see us. Let's go and see him!"

When the two chief examiners found Zhang Haogu, they said to him: "If you hadn't had the prince's card that day, you'd never have been allowed into the examination hall." Not knowing what they meant, Zhang made an ambiguous reply. After they left he was told that Prince Wei was Wei Zhongxian. He reflected that if it hadn't been for his private card, he'd never have been able to enter the examination hall and resolved to go and thank him. So he bought a great number of valuable things and went to Wei's residence. He handed in his card and a list of presents. Wei didn't recognize his name and didn't want to meet him, but he was impressed by the gifts and said, "Let him in."   On entering Zhang said to Wei, "If not for the card you gave me that night I'd never have been able to enter the examination hall.   With your assistance, I came second.   I wish to thank you." "Ah, he really is a great man of letters!" Wei was surprised.   "That's why he talked big that night.   He'll be useful to me in future when I become emperor." Presently he ordered his servants to give him a banquet. After Zhang had eaten and drunk his fill, the prince personally saw him to the door. Soon the news spread all over Beijing and shook the entire officialdom.

They said, "When we went to pay respects to Prince Wei, none of us was seen to the door by him.   But when Zhang Haogu, a new successful examination candidate, visited him, the prince did so in person." "He must be a relative or close friend." "When they were at the door, Prince Wei was very respectful to Zhang. Zhang might even be Wei's senior." "Since he is so senior, we must write a joint memorial to the throne to recommend him. When he becomes an official, he'll help us."

All agreed. "All right!" So they jointly wrote a memorial to the throne saying that the new successful candidate Zhang Haogu had great administrative ability and the will to safeguard the country and maintain order — a pillar of society. The emperor was delighted and said, "Since he is so talented, he should enter the Imperial Academy." So Zhang Haogu became an imperial academician. In the Imperial Academy, everyone knew he was sent by Prince Wei and had been recommended jointly by all officials. How could they look down upon him? When they had any memorials or documents to write, they did not let him do it but would do it for him and ask for his opinion. "Brother Zhang, what do you think of this?" they would ask.

"Great! Very good!" was his only reply. No matter what he was asked he just gave the same answer: "Great, very good!" In this way he stayed one year at the Imperial Academy.

The following year, as Wei Zhongxian's birthday was approaching, all the officials began to prepare presents for him. Zhang Haogu, after buying many valuable things, purchased a pair of scrolls and took them to the Imperial Academy. When others saw the scrolls, they asked, "Brother Zhang, is this a brithday present?" "Of course." They unfolded them and said, "They're still blank! You've been here for more than one year now, but we still haven't seen your calligraphy. Today we'll have the honour of seeing it."

No matter what he was asked he just gave the same answer: "Great, very good!" In this way he stayed one year at the Imperial Academy.

"No! No! Your handwriting is much better than mine, you'd better write it for me," he said, but all declined.

Suddenly one of them thought to himself: perhaps Zhang Haogu is illiterate, so he volunteered, "I'll write it for you." He composed two verses denouncing Wei Zhongxian's notorious activities in conspiring against the state and attempting to usurp the throne and wrote them on the scrolls. Then he asked Zhang Haogu, "Brother Zhang, what do you think of this?" "Great! Very good, very good!" came the reply.

On Wei's birthday, Zhang took the gifts and scrolls with him and went to celebrate the occasion. Wei accepted all the presents and hung the scrolls on the wall. Before he had time to read what was written on them, an imperial edict arrived. He hurriedly went out to lay an incense burner on the table to welcome the edict. Although all the officials saw the verses on the scrolls, they dared not mention it since the prince was such a merciless man. If one told him someone had cursed him, he would say, "Then both of you must die, because he cursed me and *you know* he cursed me." So who would risk his neck to tell him about the couplets? The scrolls remained on the wall for a whole day, without Wei Zhongxian noticing them.

Several years later, Emperor Chongzhen came to the throne.

Imperial robes and a crown were found in Wei Zhongxian's house and he was arrested on a charge of trying to usurp the throne. All his family members, relatives, friends and those who had connections with him were sentenced to death. Someone reported to the emperor, saying that Zhang Haogu in the Imperial Academy also belonged to Wei's clique. The emperor ordered, "Have him killed!"

But an official knelt before the emperor and said: "Your Majesty, Zhang Haogu did not belong to Wei Zhongxian's clique."

"How do you know?"

"Because he sent Wei Zhongxian a pair of couplets on his birthday. I can still remember them. The words were: In former times Cao Cao* intended to sit on the throne. The second read: Now Prince Wei wants to become an emperor. He compares Wei Zhongxian to Cao Cao, saying that he was conspiring against the state and wanted to usurp the throne. How could he belong to Wei 's clique?"

The emperor said, "I see. Then he's a loyal subject. In that case, I pardon him and promote him three grades."

And that is how the illiterate Zhang Haogu came to be a senior official.

(*Told by Liu Baorui*)

---

* Cao Cao (AD 155-220), statesman and warlord of the Three Kingdoms Period, was depicted as a treacherous court official in classical drama.

Huang the Diviner

THIS is a story about fortune-telling.

Once upon a time, a peasant by the name of Huang lived in a village not far from the capital. He had small beady eyes, flaring nostrils, a wide mouth and a face like a frog. Although odd-looking, he was quick-witted and had a glib tongue. He could read a little and would often leaf through the almanac when he had nothing better to do. He was able to choose auspicious days for weddings and house-building and the villagers held him in respect and believed everything he said.

Here is how this situation came about.

His wife had an arthritic leg which pained her when the weather changed. They could do nothing about this and by and by Huang found he could forecast the weather from it. If it hurt, it meant it would be overcast and if it hurt very badly, then it was sure to rain.

One day, in the glaring hot sun, Huang put on his woven fibre raincoat to go work in the fields. His wife stopped him.

"Are you crazy? Putting on that raincoat in such fine weather? Take it off." She reached out and cried, "Ouch, my leg."

He laughed. "See. Didn't you say your leg hurt? It's going to rain." On his way to the fields people laughed at him. "What's the matter with you, Old Huang, wearing a raincoat in the sun?"

"Nothing. It's going to rain."

No one paid any attention to him. Soon the sky became overcast, laden with black clouds. Thunder rolled and rain poured down. Everyone was drenched except Huang.

One overcast morning, Huang asked his wife, "Does your leg hurt?" "No." So he went without a raincoat while everybody else wore one.

"You don't want to be caught in the rain, do you?" the villagers asked him.

"No. But it isn't going to rain."

People were sceptical. Soon the sun came out. The day was fine, no raincoats needed.

After this had happened a few times, people began to think he knew something they didn't. So they asked him, "How do you know when it's going to rain and when it's not, Old Huang?"

"I just know."

It would have been embarrassing to have to admit that he forecast the weather by his wife's leg. Still he had to say something since he was pressed time and time again.

"Well, I predicted it," he replied.

That was how everyone came to know that he could divine and forecast the future.

When the Zhangs' daughter-in-law lost an ear-ring she went to consult him. "Uncle Huang. Can you use your powers to find it for me?" Huang pretended to count his fingers and told her, "Look around the stove and behind the water vat. You will find it there."

And she did. Old Huang thought that a daughter-in-law, cooking for the family, must be near the stove and water vat a lot of the time. Those would be the best places to look.

Brother Li had been away three months and had not written home. When was he returning? His wife sought Huang out who closed his eyes and counted his fingers, mumbling gibberish. Then he told her, "He'll be back within a month. Don't you worry."

Before ten days had passed, Li returned. As Brother Li's wife was expecting a baby that month, Huang was sure he would return.

The people who came to him were too anxious to think straight. Since many visited him for his divinations, he became known as Huang the Diviner. Though he gained fame, he made no money. His clients were friends, relatives and neighbours. The rich had no use for him. But, as luck would have it, a fortune came his way. How did it happen? A theft had been committed in the palace, a theft of a priceless pearl as big as a *longan* nut, which had the power to repel insects by day and was luminous by night. The angry emperor ordered his officials to search for it and told them if they failed to find it, they would be demoted and their salaries cut.

The officials looked everywhere they could think of but in vain. Nor were they likely to find it since it had been stolen by the Master of the Imperial Household, the one person who was in charge of it.

No one suspected him. Later that day, the emperor lost his temper in court.

"I maintain you year in year out so that you'll be useful in an emergency. But you are all good-for-nothings although you live on me. I'll take the matter in hand myself and find the thief. Master of the Household!"

The master was petrified. Had he been found out? "Your Majesty."

'Within three days, you must find a diviner to locate the pearl."

"Yes, Your Majesty." Relieved, the master excused himself, called for his horse and took a party of men to find a diviner. Soon they came to a house where a sign read, "Liu the Iron Mouth". The master dismounted and entered the house.

Liu saluted him, saying, "Do you want your fortune told?"

"Are you a good diviner?"

"Certainly. I've got an iron mouth. What I say will always come true."

"Are you positive?"

"Absolutely."

"Then I don't require your services."

The master summoned his assistants and rode off. "What a crazy official," thought Liu.

The master went to all the local diviners but wouldn't hire anyone who claimed to be good, for he didn't want one who would be able to find the thief. If he was found out he would lose his head. But of course all diviners claimed great success, otherwise how could they make a living?

The second day, the Master of the Imperial Household sought out the fortune-telling stalls asking each and every one whether or not they could make good predictions. He couldn't find a person he liked. By noon on the third day, he still hadn't found his man. His followers, not knowing what he was up to, reported, "We've gone through all the diviners in the city, my lord."

"Well. ..."

"There's someone called Huang the Diviner in the suburbs."

"Let's go to him."

Huang was feeling sorry for his wife who was groaning over the ache in her leg when the sound of horse hooves stopped outside his door and in walked the master followed by his men.

"Are you Huang the Diviner?"

"Your humble servant's name is Huang. I was given the nickname the diviner."

"Are you a good fortune-teller?"

Startled, Huang thought, "I was only teasing my neighbours and telling them nonsense. I can't predict at all." So he admitted, "It was all rubbish I was talking, my lord."

"Excellent," said the master to himself. Then he asked, "Are you sure you can't tell fortunes?"

"Absolutely."

"Wonderful." The master was overjoyed. "The luminous pearl in the palace was stolen. The emperor wants you to locate it."

Huang was scared out of his wits. How could he be a clairvoyant for the emperor? One wrong word and he was finished. He must stress that what he had said had all been rubbish.

"My lord. I dare not go. I don't make good predictions."

"That's just it. If you do, I don't want you."

"In that case I *do* make good predictions."

"What's that?"

"You'll soon see. It will rain today."

"Is that so? All the more reason for you to go."

"He's looking for an excuse," thought the master. "I have spent three days trying to find somebody who is no good. No use your pretending to be good now. I've decided on you."

Huang couldn't get away. Before he left he confided to his wife, "I'm in danger. If I act carefully, I might get out of it. If I don't show up in three days, this is what you must do. . . ."

Huang accompanied the master to the capital, was put in a hostel and told to get ready to see the emperor the following day.

In the evening, it rained. Huang was worried stiff and couldn't go to sleep. He missed his wife whose leg must be aching and who would be worried about him. What should he tell the emperor tomorrow? How could he find this luminous pearl which he had never set eyes on? Would it have found its way into a brick bed, the cattle shed, or into the kindling pile? But the palace didn't have these things.

At the end of his tether, Huang cursed the thief out loud. He gritted his teeth and scolded, "Must you steal from the emperor?"

He also hated the Master of the Imperial Household. "I told you I couldn't divine. But you dragged me here. My coming won't do you any good. You'll die a violent death."

Who could have known that the master himself would be eavesdropping outside. Having put Huang up at the hostel, he felt so good that he had supper served and was drinking wine. No one will be able to find the luminous pearl, he thought. Tomorrow, when Huang failed to do so, the emperor would fly into a rage and have him killed. Then he was saved. This man with small beady eyes, flaring nostrils and a wide mouth was ugly and uncouth. He'd never find him out.... But then, he heard a pelting sound and looked out of the window. It was raining.

"Oh no." The master's heart jumped. So Huang really could predict things. His appearance belied his ability. If tomorrow Huang divined that he was the thief, he would lose his head.

His appetite instantly disappeared. He decided to sound Huang out, ordered his horse and rode straight to the hostel. He didn't have himself announced and instead made his way stealthily to Huang's room to see what he was up to.

He was just in time to hear Huang shout, "Must you steal from the emperor?"

The Master of the Imperial Household shook in his shoes. Did he mean me, he wondered. How did he know I was here?

Then Huang said again, "I told you I wasn't clairvoyant. But you dragged me here. My coming won't do you any good. You'll die a violent death."

The Master of the Imperial Household was scared out of his wits. "He meant me! I'll die a violent death. *Aiya.* He is a good diviner after all."

He pushed open the door and threw himself at Huang's feet banging his head on the ground, pleading, "Have mercy on me. I'll tell you everything."

Although he had intended to come to sound Huang out, he gave away his own secret instead.

Shocked by his pleading Huang collected himself and helped him up saying pompously,

"D n't kowtow to me. Get up. Have no fear. I already know."

"He wants more," thought the master, who fell down on his knees. "What about a thousand taels? I'll bring them over tomorrow."

In fact, Huang was completely baffled.

The master rose quivering. "I'll tell you even though you already know. Have mercy on me, please. You're a real diviner. I've buried the pearl under a palm tree in the palace garden. If you don't tell anyone that I'm the one who took it, I'll reward you with 500 taels of silver."

The knowledge of where the pearl was had been so unexpected that Huang was both overjoyed and afraid. Overjoyed because he had found the secret, afraid because the master was a powerful man. He cleared his throat, wondering what to do.

"He wants more," thought the master, who fell down on his knees again. "What about a thousand taels? I'll bring them over tomorrow."

Reassured, Huang helped him up. "Tomorrow I am supposed to do the divination. But I'll cover up for you."

So, without doing even a stroke of work Huang was a rich man.

The following day he got up very early in the morning and went to the imperial court. After the master had made his report, Huang was summoned. Having paid his respects, he pretended to calculate on his fingers like a true diviner.

"Is there a palm tree in the palace garden, Your Majesty?"

The emperor was pleased. This rather uncouth looking individual knew that there was a palm tree in the garden!

"Yes," he said. "But I want to know where the pearl is."

"It is buried under the tree, Your Majesty."

"Let's go there."

All the officials followed the emperor to the garden. A spade and a pickaxe were brought and soon the pearl was discovered. Curious, the emperor asked, "Who stole this pearl and who buried it here?"

"Well. . . ." Huang hesitated.

The master's heart was in his mouth. Huang continued, "The luminous pearl is a state treasure. Year after year it has received the essence of the sun and moon and consequently has the power to move itself."

The master heaved a sigh of relief. The emperor was taken in. No wonder everyone thought him stupid.

The emperor rewarded him with a hundred gold ingots and ten bolts of brocade, but wouldn't grant his request to leave.

Why did he keep Huang when the treasure had been found? Many people had searched for the pearl for many days without finding it while Huang did so effortlessly. If he could have the services of this rare talent, he would know everything.

Huang was anxious to go home. He had told his wife before he left that if he didn't return in three days she was to set fire to the haystack. He would pretend to know that his house was on fire in order to escape and could be seen to be demonstrating his divining powers at the same time.

On the third morning he was on the point of asking the master to take him to the emperor when he was summoned. He quietly told the emperor, "I felt anxious and had a vision. My house is on fire, Your Majesty. Please let me go home to see to things."

The emperor was reluctant to let him go. How could he know that his house was on fire when it was dozens of *li* away. He would send men to check first and if it was true he would give him a title and keep him in court.

"Don't worry about it. Let's have a feast with my favourite officials."

His word was law. Huang had to accept and drink with him however worried he might be.

The emperor sent out a rider and Huang thought, "If my wife has set fire to the haystack, there's a chance of my going home. But if she should begrudge the loss and disobey my orders, I'm done for."

Huang drank some wine but was too worried to eat much. When the feast was over, the man returned and confirmed that Huang's house had indeed burnt down. The emperor declared, "You are truly clairvoyant. Don't worry. I'll look after you and grant you the title of Guardian of the State for your talents. You'll stay here with my officials and lead a luxurious life."

Huang didn't want to be a palace diviner. He refused saying, "I'm just a country bumpkin, quite unsuitable for court life. Your Majesty had better give the title to a qualified man."

"Please don't refuse."

"But I can't accept it."

"Why?"

"I'm destined to misfortune if I become an official."

"Is that so?"

Annoyed, the emperor mused, "So you don't want to serve me. If you should serve others, my safety would be in danger."

The emperor thought of a wicked plan. "Come,

Master of the Imperial Household. I'll tell you something."

He whispered instructions and the master left, returning shortly with a box. He stood beside the emperor.

The emperor told Huang, "Inside this box is a rare treasure. I'll have a joss-stick lit. If you can tell me what it is before the joss-stick burns out, you can go home. Otherwise you will be punished for deceiving the emperor."

That placed Huang in a dilemma. There were so many rare treasures in the palace which he couldn't even name so how could he guess at random? But death was certain if he made a wrong guess. He had only one life to lose. If he made no guesses at all, he was sure to die anyway. What could he do?

The joss-stick was almost finished. Everybody had their eyes on Huang. Once the emperor gave the order he would be killed. In a cold sweat, Huang stamped his foot and sighed, "I never expected Froggy to be trapped by a box."

The emperor gasped. So did the Master of the Imperal Household. When the box was opened the officials saw that a gold frog inlaid with jade had been placed inside. It had small beady eyes, flaring nostrils, a wide mouth and a big belly.

It so happened that when he was a child, Huang's parents had nicknamed him Froggy and, quite by chance it was this name that he had blurted out in exasperation.

And that is how Huang the Diviner made his fortune.

(*Told by Zhang Shouchen*)

Pearl-Emerald-Jade Soup

WHEN Zhu Hongwu raised troops to overthrow the Yuan Dynasty, he and his lieutenants Chang Yuchun and Hu Dahai charged into the military drill-ground in Beijing. But the Partriarch Tatar had buried mines there, and tht rebels had to flee the city and scatter Zhu rode off alone, taking to the wilds, cold and hungry, till he and his horse were worn out. Finally he dismounted beside a small tumble-down temple, where he lost consciousness and fell to the ground.

Some time later along came two beggars, one with a battered wicker crate of stale buns and flapjacks, the other with a chipped earthenware pot of vegetable soup. At the entrance to the temple they saw a man lying there like a dead pig. Finding that he was still breathing, they carried him into the temple. Then they fetched twigs and straw to light a fire and laid Zhu beside it, cross-legged, to bring him round.

The smoke brought him to his senses, but he was so dazed that he thought his own men were still with him.

"Brother Chang!" he called to Chang Yuchun.

One of tht beggars thought, "Strange! I don't know him, yet he's calling my name."

Then Zhu Hongwu called, "Here!"*

---

* The character *lai* for "here" is also a surname.

The other beggar thought, "Odd! He knows my name too."

The other beggar thought, "Odd! He knows my name too."

It was sheer coincidence.

Zhu pointed to his mouth, "I'm famished!"

It dawned on the beggars that he wasn't ill, just hungry. They knew from their own experience how wretched it is to go hungry. All right, they would go short themselves and give him something to eat. They warmed up their vegetable soup on the fire and gave it to Zhu Hongwu, who was so ravenous that he wolfed it down. After gulping down that soup, he broke into a sweat. Fine! He felt much better.

He asked the two beggars their names.

"Didn't you know my name's Chang Xiandi?"*

"Oh, so you're Brother Chang."

Before he got round to asking if they had been wounded, he realized his mistake. So he said, "What's the name of that soup you just gave me?"

They thought: It was just left over. If he wants us to give it a name, let's call it "pearl-emerald-jade soup". How come? Well, the cabbage and spinach leaves were like emeralds, the rancid beancurd like jade, and the bits of rice crust like pearls. Right!

"It's pearl-emerald-jade soup."

Zhu Hongwu nodded. "Thank you." He rode off.

Later Zhu Hongwu did topple the Yuan Dynasty and became emperor in Nanjing. He lived off the fat of the land, dressed in silks and brocades in a magnificent palace, reigning as an absolute ruler whose word was law. If he said that coal was white, who dared contradict him? If he said "Fools are good", fools would

---

* *Xiandi* can also mean "worthy younger brother".

have to be promoted three ranks. If he gave a minister a sheet of toilet paper, it would have to be mounted on yellow silk and displayed in the hall as a treasure.

When Zhu Hongwu had been emperor for a few years, he grew tired of that life of luxury. In his boredom he felt as limp as he had years ago in that tumbledown temple. He issued an order: "Here! Tell the cooks to make me a bowl of pearl-emerald-jade soup."

When a eunuch passed on this order the cooks were filled with consternation.

Master Zhang asked Master Li, "Do you know how to make this soup?"

"No, I don't."

"Master Wang?"

"I've never heard of it either. I know you can soften pearls by steaming them; but how do you chop up emerald and jade?"

"If we don't make it but disobey the emperor's orders, we're done for!"

To save their skins they tried to muddle through. They took a few big pearls and steamed them for several hours, then found some fragments of emerald and jade, to which they added some soup stock and coriander. They asked a young eunuch to serve this, begging him:

"Put in a good word for us with the emperor!"

The eunuch carried in this bowl of soup. It looked splendid, so white and green, and when Zhu Hongwu stirred it with his spoon it tinkled. But it didn't taste right. He flew into a rage.

"What's this?"

"Pearl-emerald-jade soup."

"Bosh! I've had pearl-emerald-jade soup before."

The young eunuch rushed back in dismay to the imperial kitchen. "Watch out!"

"What's wrong?" asked the cooks.

"The emperor says he's had pearl-emerald-jade soup before. This soup of yours isn't right."

The cooks exclaimed, "Now we're for it! This is not just failing to carry out the imperial orders, we're committing high treason."

Since they couldn't hope to get by, they decided to admit that they didn't know how to make this soup and to beg the emperor to find someone who could. The young eunuch reported this. Zhu Hongwu reflected: Yes, my cooks are used to cooking delicacies, so I can't blame them if they can't make this. But I must have that soup! Not just for myself, I'll treat everyone in the palace and all my ministers to it. Thereupon he issued an edict, which was posted up everywhere, to find those two men who could make pearl-emerald-jade soup. One was called Chang Xiandi, he'd forgotten the name of the other.

This imperial edict was posted up everywhere, including the county town where Zhu Hongwu had nearly come to grief. One day the two beggars were going from door to door there when they saw a crowd of people reading a notice on the screen-wall outside the yamen. They went over to ask what it was. The emperor was looking for Chang Xiandi and another man whose name he didn't know, to make him pearl-emerald-jade soup.

"Well!" they exclaimed. "So that fellow who drank our left-over vegetable soup is the emperor! We must go and see him."

They tore off the imperial edict. When two yamen runners saw this they arrested them.

"What's up?" the beggars asked. "Going to take us in chains to make soup for the emperor?"

The runners apologized, "Sorry, gentlemen! We didn't know. Excuse us!"

"That's all right," said the beggars.

"Please go to the yamen, gentlemen."

"Where's the carriage?"

"It's just here, the yamen. We'll carry you on our backs."

The people standing by wondered. Why are they carrying beggars into the yamen?

The runners carried them into the lock-up.

"First rest here, gentlemen, while we announce this to the magistrate."

The two runners hurried in to report this. The magistrate thought: I ought to be promoted for finding these two fellows. He promptly changed into new official robes and, all spruced up, went out respectfully to the hall to receive them.

The two runners rushed out to announce, "Gentlemen, our magistrate's waiting for you in the hall."

"All right, lead the way."

"Very good."

The two beggars muttered, "That's right, we must stand on our dignity."

When the magistrate saw them he coudn't understand why these beggars had been brought in.

The runners said, "Your Excellency, here are the two gentlemen."

The magistrate thought it strange that they should

show such respect to two barefoot beggars with filthy faces, in rags.

"Are these the men who tore down the imperial edict?" he asked.

"Yes, these are the two gentlemen."

"When can we go to the capital?" asked the beggars.

The magistrate thought they were having him on. He was furious. How could fellows like this make pearl-emerald-jade soup? He didn't believe it! But suppose he was guilty of deceiving the emperor by not taking them there, and the emperor found out, he'd have to pay with his life.. How unfair it would be if he lost his post because of these two beggars. He couldn't risk it.

"Here!" he ordered. "Chain them up and we'll escort them to the capital."

When the emperor heard of their arrival he thought: So I've really found them. He summoned them to his presence. The magistrate brought them to the court in chains, and knelt down at the foot of the dais to pay homage. He'd never been in such a place before and was trembling with fright like a sieve sieving chaff. But he saw out of the corner of his eyes that the beggars were grinning and nodding at the emperor. Why was that? The emperor recognized the two men who had saved his life. He thought: What a fool this magistrate is, not fitting them out decently to see me! What will my officials think if I say I know these beggars?

"Why are you got up like that, my good fellows?" he asked.

"This is our usual get-up," they answered. "Only now we've these chains as well."

At once Zhu Hongwu swore at the magistrate, "You

idiot, how dare you chain the men I've invited to make pearl-emerald-jade soup? Just asking for trouble! Take him out, off with his head!"

The two beggars thought this was letting him off too lightly! They told the emperor, "Do spare his life, Your Majesty, and let him help us buy the ingredients for our pearl-emerald-jade soup." Ha!

Zhu Hongwu agreed to this. He gave them three hundred taels to set up a new kitchen, and ordered them to make two hundred helpings of pearl-emerald-jade soup. Three days later he would feast his ministers.

The three of them withdrew to the new kitchen. At once the magistrate knelt down and said, "Thank you, gentlemen, for saving my life."

"Forget it. Go and buy us our ingredients."

"Yes, just tell me what you want. We must carry out the emperor's orders. You are dab hands and, brainless as I am, I can buy the very best of any of the delicacies you need. When I've made a good job of it, with the emperor's favour and the help of you two gentlemen I hope I shall be promoted four or five ranks."

The beggars thought: Fine. You've just escaped execution and you're dreaming of promotion and making a fortune. "Stop talking rubbish," they told him, "and go shopping."

"Yes, yes."

"Go on. Buy four hundred pounds of beancurd, five hundred of spinach with roots, five hundred of the outer leaves of cabbage, three hundred of coarse rice, ten of crude salt, five of sand, half a pound of soot and forty buckets of dishwater. That should do us."

"What do you want that junk for?"

"Don't quibble, just do as we say. If you leave anything out and it's not to the emperor's taste, you'll have to answer for it. So get cracking."

"Right."

Soon everything was bought except for the outer cabbage leaves and dishwater. To get these the magistrate had to go with two buckets and a crate to different restaurants.

In two days all the ingredients were ready. The beggars inspected them. "This won't do. The spinach is too fresh, the beancurd isn't rancid, the emperor won't find it to his liking and you'll be the one to blame."

The terrified magistrate knelt down and kowtowed. "Please think of a way out for me, gentlemen!"

"Tomorrow the emperor is giving a feast for all his ministers. You haven't bought the right ingredients, and we're short-handed, so what's to be done?"

"Never mind," said the magistrate. "Rope in three cooks from the imperial kitchen."

Those three cooks were delighted when told to help prepare pearl-emerald-jade soup.

One said, "Here's a fine chance to learn. We don't want this skill to be lost."

Another said, "Quite right. We must learn well from them."

The two beggars said, "Now we'll make pearl-emerald-jade soup." They told two of the cooks to boil the rice over a slow fire. "Mind! Don't wash the rice. And we don't want the rice from the top, only the crust from the bottom of the pan."

"What do they want that for?" wondered one of the cooks.

"Never mind," said the other. "We're here to learn from them, aren't we?"

The beggars told the magistrate, "Don't sit idle. Steep that beancurd in the dishwater and mash it up, then sun it until it ferments."

"Right."

There was still another cook.

"You come and help us sort through this spinach. The good leaves must be thrown away, the rotten roots kept."

These instructions bewildered the magistrate and the three cooks. "What on earth are they trying to do?"

They worked all night. The next morning, the magistrate and the three cooks sat there looking blankly at the rotten spinach, burnt rice crust, outer cabbage leaves and rancid beancurd. When the sun came out the dishwater smelt putrid.

The cooks asked the magistrate, "Your Excellency, when are we going to make pearl-emerald-jade soup?"

"Don't ask me!" growled the magistrate. "Ask these two gentlemen."

The two beggars, hearing this, pointed at the buckets and said, "Isn't this pearl-emerald-jade soup? We've done seven tenths of the job. When the emperor's drunk this soup he will reward us."

Reward them, the others thought! We can only hope he doesn't sack us. What sort of feast is this for his ministers — rotten vegetables, burnt rice and stinking soup? We'd better look out! We'll be lucky if our homes aren't raided.

They saw the beggars scoop out some soup to taste it. "Not bad, this is something like it."

One fished out a morsel of beancurd from the bottom

of the bucket and popped it in his mouth. "Good! Tastes fine." He slapped the magistrate on the shoulder. "You're the one who prepared the beancurd. My brother and I will tell the emperor, and you should win promotion and get rich."

The magistrate thought: Heaven help me!

It would soon be time for the feast. The beggars told the cooks and the magistrate to heat up the soup, add salt and put in some handfuls of sand. Finding it not gritty enough they added more sand.

One said, "It's not dark enough."

"Where's the soot?" asked the other.

Right, they emptied in a big packet of soot and tasted the soup again. When it boiled, the rancid smell nearly choked the magistrate and cooks.

"Good," said the beggars. "Dish it up and serve it."

That day the palace was brightly lit and decked out. The emperor's relatives and ministers had all arrived at the crack of dawn to wait for this treat — pearl-emerald-jade soup.

One said, "This pearl-emerald-jade soup is really special. Once the emperor did my father the favour of letting him taste it. When he came home he sang its praises. Now I'm to have this honour too, I'm really in luck."

Another said, "I've heard that it's made of dragon liver, phoenix marrow and all kinds of rare delicacies. Preparing it is a long business, a unique soup like this."

When the feast started, young eunuchs lined up holding gilded vermilion boxes in which were bowls with dragon designs from the imperial kilns. And in each bowl was a helping of pearl-emerald-jade soup. All the guests were impressed by the punctilious way the eunuchs had turned their faces away, not presuming to look at the soup. The first bowl was offered to the emperor. When he sniffed it he felt rather nauseated, but the smell reminded him of that soup he had drunk in the tumble-down temple which had made him feel so good! He had been longing to taste it again — why did it smell so bad today? No wonder people say, "To the starving, husks taste sweet as honey. To the replete honey isn't sweet enough." The emperor thought to himself, "I was famished then, now I'm living in luxury. Still I drank this once and ought to drink it again. Not only me, I must make everybody drink it."

Zhu Hongwu looked down from his dais and saw frowns on the faces of all his guests as they stared at the soup. That made him furious. He thought: You're going to share this treat with me! That's right! We'll drink this together.

He said, "My dear ministers, set to! Drink this pearl-emerald-jade soup with me." He gulped his down, nearly choking.

When this rancid soup had been served to the guests they thought: Not even we can drink this, not to say the emperor. Those two fellows who made it should be cut to pieces. Now they were astounded to see the emperor lap it up. At once they gulped theirs down too. Some of them wanted to spit it out, it tasted so foul, but they dared not do that in the imperial presence — that would have been high treason. So, holding their breath they swallowed it mouthful by mouthful. All of them managed somehow to finish their bowls.

When Zhu Hongwu saw they had finished, he asked with a smile, "Well, dear ministers, what do you think

All sprang to their feet to express their humble thanks.

"Delicious, delicious," they cried.

"In that case," said the emperor, "you'll each have two more bowls."

of this pearl-emerald-jade soup I summoned men to prepare?"

All sprang to their feet to express their humble thanks.

"Delicious, delicious," they cried.

"In that case," said the emperor, "you'll each have two more bowls."

That was really the last straw!

(*Told by Zhang Shouchen*)

Three Blows in One Day

THE hardest thing about *xiangsheng* is not knowing what the audience wants to hear. Some have literary tastes, some like stories about fighting. Not only do their tastes differ, so do their temperaments. Some people have such quick tempers, they glare at you and can't talk civilly. Others are such slowcoaches, they never get worked up. If a quick-tempered man meets a slow-coach that's just too bad. He may die of rage.

"Just come?" a slowcoach once asked to make conversation.

"Yes, just come," Quick-Temper snapped back.

"Why are you in such a temper?"

"The sight of you makes me mad."

"You needn't look at me then."

"Did I come here to see you? If you go on pestering me I'll wallop you."

"Wallop me? I'd have to see it to believe it."

"I'll give you a walloping. Do you believe me?"

"No. It's flat here, see. Why not try."

This made Quick-Temper so mad, he punched him hard. Anyone else would have fought back before he was punched again. But Slowcoach only smiled.

"I didn't believe them when they said you beat people. Now I've seen it with my own eyes. Why not punch me on this side as well to even things up."

Quick-Temper shook his fist. "Bah! You're the limit!" He went away fuming.

Another type of character is always on the make. If he can't buy at bargain prices he feels bad. One man like this took a copper to the grocer's. Other people could only buy one thing for a copper, but he got six. He went in and smiled at the grocer.

"Had your breakfast?"

The sight of him irritated any shopkeeper, but the grocer had to serve him.

"What can I get for you?"

"I'm eating noodles today."

"Never mind what you're eating. What can I get for you?"

"Half a copper's worth of soya sauce and half a copper's worth of vinegar."

The grocer got these for him.

"And a drop of sesame oil from that vat, as flavouring."

He got that drop of sesame oil — three things.

"And throw in a few scallion leaves, will you?" That made four.

"And a pinch of coriander." That made five. When the grocer turned to get him the coriander, he filched two heads of garlic — that made six. A fellow like that is a pain in the neck.

This reminds me of a story. Once there was a newly-appointed magistrate. When he went to his post and took his seat in the court, his runners and bailiffs lined up respectfully on both sides. He called two bailiffs out to ask:

"What's the situation here?"

"Very orderly, Your Honour. No robbers or brigands here."

"Well, I want you to make three arrests: A man with a quick temper, a slowcoach and someone on the make. I give you seven days. If you succeed I'll reward you; if you fail I'll come down on you hard. Off you go!"

The more they thought about it, the less the bailiffs liked this assignment. Robberies were easy to handle, but where could they find a man with a quick temper? They could hardly stop people in the street to ask:

"Are you quick-tempered?"

"What gives you that idea?"

"Are you a slowcoach?"

"You're the slowcoach."

"Are you on the make?"

"No, that's you."

They didn't know what to do. Seven days later they were given forty strokes each. They were then allowed another seven days in which to make the three arrests. Again they failed and received forty strokes. Then they were given another seven days. By now they were thoroughly exasperated.

As they left the yamen one said, "This is an impossible assignment, brother. We can't ask for leave or quit — he wouldn't let us. We'll just have to stick it out. Let's go and get drunk."

They were drinking in a tavern when they saw a crowd of people in the street, all heading west. They asked the tavern keeper, "What's happened today to attract such a crowd?"

He told them, "While you gentlemen were in the yamen these people were handing in their petitions. Now they're going outside the West Gate to sacrifice to the God of Green Shoots and put on an opera in gratitude for a good harvest. They're all off to watch the opera."

One bailiff suggested, "Brother, let's go too."

The other said, "Come off it. A few more days and we'll be lambasted again. I'm in no mood for an opera."

"It's no use worrying. Let's enjoy ourselves while we can."

They paid for their drinks and walked out of the town chatting.

In those days there were no seats for operas put on in the countryside. The audience had to stand. If you wanted to sit down you could bring a stool from home, but then you had to lug it back again. The bailiffs joined the crowd of spectators just as a general was fighting the enemy in the opera and a quarrel started in the audience. A slowcoach in the front row was cheering. What a sight he was, arms akimbo, swaying from side to side and wagging his head. "Bravo, bravo!" he exclaimed. A hothead behind him let out a yell that nearly bowled him over. "Fine!"

Slowcoach looked round. "Trying to burst your lungs? Just applaud and have done with it. Why yell like that?"

"What I do is none of your business."

"Must I steer clear of you?"

Just then a boy came running up from outside to grab the hand of Slowcoach. "Dad! Our house is on fire, dad!"

"On fire, eh? You go home first, I'll come when this opera's finished."

That made Quick-Temper see red. He lashed out and knocked Slowcoach down. "Call yourself a man?

Your house is on fire. You should hurry home. If you wait till the opera's over, the fire will spread to other people's houses."

Lying on the ground Slowcoach answered, "It's *my* house, none of your business. If I feel like it I'll go home after this opera. If I don't feel like it, I'll go home two weeks from now."

"How maddening you are. I'll kill you!"

"Fine, that would save me the trouble of getting up."

Someone standing beside them objected, "You're making such a row that we can't hear." Then he spotted the two bailiffs. "Oh, officers, look at these men kicking up such a row."

The bailiffs came over and asked, "How did this start?"

"Ask him!" said Quick-Temper.

Slowcoach was still lying on the ground. The bailiffs said, "Get up, you!"

"I'm not getting up."

"Why not?"

"If I get up he'll knock me down again."

"Not with us here, he wouldn't dare."

Slowcoach got up and dusted off his clothes.

The bailiffs asked again, "How did this start?"

"I was watching the opera when my son came to tell me our house is on fire. I said I'd go back after the opera. Then this man hit me so hard he nearly killed me."

"What a rum fellow you are! Why not go home at once to put out the fire? If you wait till after the opera, suppose it spreads to your neighbours' houses?"

"Well, the fact is I was born a slowcoach like this."

"Good," said the bailiffs. "Because of you we've been given eighty strokes." They took out a clanking chain and chained him up. Then they told Quick-Temper, "You had no right to hit him."

"He made me mad."

"Still you shouldn't have hit him."

"That's the way I am — quick-tempered."

The bailiffs chained him up too.

"Hey! What are you doing? I'll leave him alone, all right?"

"Nothing doing. Those eighty strokes were because of you too."

As the bailiffs led their prisoners off they thought: Well, this trip paid off, two men nabbed. But that won't do: we're still short of someone on the make. Soon they came to a pedlar's stall where two men were wrangling.

The customer asked, "Are these melon seeds of yours fried?" He popped two into his mouth. "Are these peanuts spiced? Still crisp?" He tasted everything.

The pedlar said, "No need to buy anything, you've already stuffed yourself."

"Who says I'm not buying? How much are these sweets?"

"One cent each."

"How about one cent for two?"

"Nothing doing."

"Well, why glare at me like that?" He paid him a cent, reached out and took two sweets between his second and third and his fourth and fifth fingers. He had made such a nuisance of himself eating this, that and the other that the pedlar was on his guard. He grabbed his wrist.

"You can't have two."

The customer thrust both sweets into his mouth.

"Who says I can't? I've swallowed them."

"Then you must pay for them."

"You can have my life, but I've no money for you. What can you do about it!"

Just then the pedlar saw the two bailiffs with their two prisoners.

"Officers!" he called. "Please come here."

They went to his stall.

"What's up?"

"See this customer of mine? He's been tasting all my wares, not buying any. These sweets are one cent each. He paid a cent and ate two."

The bailiffs said, "A pedlar doesn't make much. How can he afford to let you take two sweets?"

"Fact is, I have to get a bargain no matter where I'm shopping, not just here. Otherwise I feel bad."

"What makes you do that?"

"I was born that way."

The two bailiffs were very pleased. They whipped out another chain and chained him up.

"Let me off, officers, and I'll change my ways."

"Nothing doing. Come with us."

The bailiffs hauled their prisoners off to the yamen and left them in the lock-up while they went in to report. At once the magistrate took his seat in court, his runners ranged on both sides.

"Bring in the prisoners," he ordered.

The three men were brought in and knelt down.

The magistrate pointed at Slowcoach and demanded, "What have you been up to?"

Slowcoach looked at him. "Your Honour, I was

listening to an opera outside town when my son came and told me that our house was on fire. I said I'd go back after the opera, then this fellow here hit me so hard he nearly killed me."

"Why didn't you hurry home to put out the fire?"

"I always dawdle, Your Honour."

The magistrate pointed at the quick-tempered man. "How can you go around beating people up?"

"Your Honour, if he didn't hurry home to put out the fire, wouldn't it burn down other houses too?"

"Still you shouldn't have hit him."

"Couldn't help it, I'm quick-tempered."

The magistrate pointed at the man on the make. "And you?"

"I have this weakness, Your Honour. I feel bad if I don't get a good bargain when I'm shopping."

The magistrate said, "Fine. Do you know why I've had you brought here?"

The three of them answered together, "No, Your Honour."

"Would you like to work for me?"

The two bailiffs hearing this were furious. They'd been given eighty strokes, gone to such trouble to find these men, and now they would be working in the yamen!

The magistrate told Quick-Temper, "You're to be my escort, that way I'll never be late. You, Slowcoach, are to look after my sons. Then no matter how they pester you, you won't lose your temper. You, Haggler, are to do my shopping for me and get me bargains."

It dawned on everyone then that this magistrate was on the make himself.

But in fact the magistrate lost out by taking on these

three men. One day he had to go out to meet a superior, and he ordered Quick-Temper to prepare his horse, but the fellow couldn't saddle it, as he was not its groom and the horse didn't know him. It kept moving away, left or right.

"Hell!" he fumed. "I'm going to get the better of you!" He fetched a chaff-cutter from the barn and chopped off the horse's head. When it had dropped dead he saddled it easily. "Well, that's that!" he chortled.

The magistrate arrived then all spruced up. "Ah! Why kill the horse?" he demanded.

"That was the only way to saddle it."

"All right, you've saddled it, but how can I ride it? If you make me late, you dolt, I'll be punished for it. Want to ruin me, do you?"

"Well, that's the way I'm made. If you don't want me to work for you I'll leave."

"All right, it's my fault for taking you on. Fetch a carriage."

The magistrate got into the carriage and Quick-Temper drove it out of town to the stream. The mule was afraid of water and balked at the ford.

"See how you're holding me up," the magistrate raged. "That horse would have crossed, this mule is afraid of water. And if we go the long way round that will make me late for my appointment."

"Don't blame the mule," said Quick-Temper. "She's afraid of water, I'm not. I'll carry you over to go and see to your business. Then I'll drive the carriage the long way round to wait for you."

"All right," said the magistrate.

Quick-Temper crouched down and hoisted the

magistrate on to his back to ford the stream. He had just reached the middle when the magistrate thought: It's good of him to carry me like this through such deep water. He said, "I'm not going to punish you for killing the horse. Instead I shall give you twenty taels of silver for carrying me over this stream."

"Thank you, Your Honour." He let go, and the magistrate fell plop into the stream. He nearly drowned!

"Why drop me in the stream?" the magistrate swore.

"I clasped my hands to thank you."

"Why not wait till we'd crossed the stream to thank me?"

"You didn't wait till we'd crossed the stream to reward me."

Well, let's face it, thought the magistrate. I haven't attended to my official duties, and now I'm like a drowned rat.

"Let's go back!" he said.

Back in the yamen the magistrate went home to change his clothes. He saw Slowcoach sunning himself in the courtyard and called to him. Slowcoach looked at him without a word.

"Didn't you hear me call you?"

"Yes, I heard."

"Why didn't you answer?"

"I looked at you, didn't I?"

"Bah, that's no way to answer. Where are the young masters?"

"Which one do you mean?"

"Where's the elder?"

"He's at school, isn't he?"

"And the younger?"

"Fallen in the well."

"Why buy two?"

"We can leave the big one here for the time being. Then we won't have to buy another when the elder young master dies."

"What! When did he fall in?"

"First thing this morning."

"Why didn't you tell me?"

"What's the hurry? I was going to tell you in a few day's time."

"You'll be the death of me! Fish him out, quick!"

When people had fished the dead child out, the magistrate sobbed, "He was such a sweet little boy, everybody loved him. Ah! We must buy a coffin." He sent Haggler of all people to buy a coffin.

In the coffin shop Haggler priced every coffin there.

"How much is this?"

"A hundred and sixty taels," said the shopkeeper.

"That one?"

"Two hundred eighty."

"This?"

"Eighty."

"And this?"

The shopkeeper asked, "How many people have died that you want to price all my coffins?"

He pointed at a casket. "How much is this?"

"Twenty taels."

"Twenty taels! Cut up for firewood how many pounds would it weigh?"

"Coffins aren't the same as firewood. Are you buying or not?"

"Of course I am. Will you sell it for ten taels?"

"There's no bargaining in coffin shops."

"How about twelve?"

"Go to some other shop."

"Thirteen."

"I'm not selling to you."

"Fourteen."

"No."

"Fourteen and a half."

"Didn't I tell you to go somewhere else?"

"Make it fifteen — how about that?"

The shopkeeper was so exasperated, he said, "All right, fifteen."

Haggler produced twenty taels. "Give me the change."

While the shopkeeper was fetching the change Haggler put a little coffin inside the big one. Then he took his change and carried the two coffins, one inside the other, to the yamen.

The magistrate was complaining, "What's taking him so long?"

He came in and announced, "I'm back," and put down the coffins.

The magistrate was furious. "Why buy such a big one? Think of all the padding we'll need to prevent the child's skin from being rubbed off."

"Don't worry, Your Honour. Here's another small one."

The magistrate flew into a rage. "Why buy two?"

"We can leave the big one here for the time being. Then we won't have to buy another when the elder young master dies."

(Told by Zhao Airu)

Born in the Year of the Ox

THINGS are very different now from the old days, when men wanted to live as parasites. Today work is honourable. Those who won't work can't earn their living. It's no good nowadays to hope to become an official and make a lot of money. In the old days those who wanted to make a fortune all tried to become officials. Why was that? Because once you became an official you got rich. When parents taught their children they poisoned their minds. A father would pat his son on the back and say, "You must land an official post, sonny, and restore the family's fortunes." Just think, how could he do that without raking money in? There was an old saying, "In three years an honest prefect makes a hundred thousand taels of silver." A hundred thousand taels in three years, and an honest prefect at that! So how much would a dishonest official make? And how did honest officials come by so much money? By embezzlement? Not by embezzlement. A prefect belonged to the fourth rank, so his salary was small. Well then, where did those hundred thousand taels come from? They had their channels.

The prefect was in charge of a number of magistrates. Each county had a magistrate, but the counties themselves varied, some having poor soil, some rich. Let's not talk about distant parts where no one has been but about some counties near us here in Tianjin, which every-body knows. They say, "Golden Baodi and silver Wu-qing aren't up to the fifth watch in Ninghe." Ask any-one over forty and what will he tell you? Baodi was a goldmine, a county of more than one thousand two hundred villages, where the magistrate made a pile. Wuqing was a silvermine, a county of eight hundred and eighty-eight villages; so in years of good harvests it provided a large income. Yet neither of these coun-ties was up to Ninghe. At the fifth watch, the crack of dawn, in Ninghe, the magistrate there made more than all the pickings in Wuqing and Baodi. Why was that? Ninghe produced salt; that salt made it a lucra-tive post. All these counties came under the jurisdic-tion of the prefect in Beijing.

Beijing had five prefectures and nineteen counties. All alike? No, very different. Baoding County in the south later had its name changed to Xinjin. The in-come from the eighteen villages there was not enough for petty cash, so the prefect's source of revenue there was small. But he didn't have to rake in money him-self, just told the magistrate to rake some in so as to sweeten him up. Ninghe County had a big income, didn't it, but its magistrate had to keep on the right side of the prefect; otherwise he'd be transferred. The prefect might switch the magistrates of Xinjin County and Ninghe. That would suit the magistrate of Xinjin fine, getting such a lucrative post, but how could the magistrate of Ninghe stand it? To prevent this he had to give presents to the prefect. He couldn't give him money, though. That would have been bribery, and if the Imperial Censor learned of it that would be the end of them both. What was to be done? All the prefect need do was to celebrate two birthdays every year, his own and his wife's. When his birthday was coming up his subordinates went to his office to ask:

"It will soon be His Honour's birthday, eh?"

"Right."

"How much. . . ."

"Well. . . ."

"What would His Honour like me to give him?"

"How do I know? Give him whatever you like."

"How old is His Honour?"

"Fifty-six."

Fifty-six, what would be an appropriate gift? Let's think. Ah, if he was fifty-six he was born in the year of the Rat. Well, go to the goldsmith's and order a rat made of a bar of gold one inch thick, weighing sixteen ounces. This rat was one foot two inches long, and its tail alone took more than one bar of gold, while its eyes were two diamonds, over five carats each. This gold rat was put on the table for birthday presents and the magistrate stood beside it staring at it, to attract the prefect's attention. From time to time the prefect would stroll in, stroking his beard, to inspect his gifts. He spotted the rat at once! Stroking his beard he weighed it in his hand. If he found it too light, just gold-plated, he would have put it down again. He weighed it in his hand and knew it was alright. When he read the name of the donor, he patted the magistrate's shoulder.

"Fine, fine. I really like this."

This meant: Don't worry, you can stay put, I won't be transferring you. He said, "The craftsmanship is really superb."

Work it out! One year younger, the year of the Ox. How much would a gold ox cost!

What did he care about the craftsmanship? It was the weight he liked!

"Well now, that was thoughtful of you, working out that I was born in the year of the Rat and having this gold rat made for me, aha! Yes, that was very thoughtful. By the way, it's my wife's birthday next month — she's a year younger than I am."

Work it out! One year younger, the year of the Ox. How much would a gold ox cost! How did he expect the common people to live?!

(Told by Zhang Shouchen)

The Miser

IT happened in our village, the strange story you're going to hear.

A big landlord here had three sons and three daughters-in-law. They owned six dozen head of cattle, some two hundred acres of farmland and two grain shops, yet they always mixed bran with their rice and instead of frying their vegetables simply boiled them in water. A big pan of vegetables, outer leaves, roots and all, with a great handful of salt — ugh! If oil was added it had to be done by the old landlord himself. What with family and servants they had over fifty mouths to feed, so how much oil do you suppose was added to this pan of vegetables? Four tenths of an ounce a day. Four ounces in ten days, right? A chopstick was kept in the oil vat with a small scoop on one end. When the master added oil, one hand on the vat, the other holding the chopstick, he scooped it up and emptied it into the pan — that was four tenths of an ounce. But strange to say, four ounces of sesame oil bought on New Year's Eve would last for a whole year, and there'd be seven and a half ounces left over — he'd produced an extra three and a half ounces! How come? Each time he emptied his scoop he refilled it with the water in the pan!

The whole household had to eat bran with him. His three daughters-in-law came from rich families and were accustomed to living well. How could they eat bran muffins? Yet they couldn't just sit there watching the old man stuffing himself with bran muffins at each meal. His sons, daughters-in-law and grandchildren had to swallow a couple of mouthfuls of muffin too, after which they put them down saying they had had enough. There were always a lot left over, and he would say gleefully:

"We're none of us big eaters, that's why our family's thriving."

After breakfast he would go off to collect horse-dung, trudging forty *li* there and back. As soon as he left there was a great clatter of cleavers and ladles in the kitchen as the others prepared to gorge themselves. Masses of meat they had and lashings of liquor. By the time he came back they had finished, cleared everything away, and his sons and their wives had enjoyed a good siesta. In the evening, when bran muffins were served again, they ate only one mouthful each.

One summer day when the miser went out after breakfast to collect dung, they prepared their meal with a clatter of cleavers and ladles. But their luck had run out — the old fellow came back early. My, if he came in and saw all that meat and liquor, there would be the devil to pay! What could they do? Don't worry, he couldn't come in, or at least only through the main gate, not through the inner gate. Why, was the inner gate locked? No. But his sons and daughters-in-law thought up a dodge. One of them took two handfuls of soya beans and scattered these by the gate. Then they could cook and eat their meal in peace, and the old man wouldn't disturb them. Why not? When he stepped through the main gate with his crate of dung, he saw beans all over the ground and let out a bellow:

"Hell! What a waste! What fool did this?"

They let him curse and swear, paying no attention as he squatted down to pick up those beans one by one. Figure it out for yourselves. By the time he had picked up every single bean the people inside had washed up.

And afterwards? He hoarded his wealth right up to the time of his death. And on his death-bed what worried him was the fear that his sons would squander his property. He called them in and asked his eldest son:

"I'm done for. How will you manage my funeral?"

His eldest son thought it too bad that his father had made so much money yet never spent it. Now he and his brothers would each inherit a share — it didn't seem right.

"Don't you worry, dad," he said. "We'll give you a handsome funeral."

"That won't do. What do you mean by handsome? Tell me."

"We've got it all worked out. We'll give you a coffin of the best *nanmu* wood. We can sell those two grain shops to pay for the funeral, can't we? You'll have a gold bed sheet below, and a silvery quilt embroidered with charms above, seven gold coins to keep down the earth, seven pearls to wear. And for forty-nine whole days we'll get Buddhists, Taoists, lamas and nuns to recite masses for you. You'll have sixty-four pall-bearers...."

Before he could say any more his father cut in, "You silly ass! What rubbish you talk. Are we made of money? Selling two grain shops wouldn't raise enough to give me such a send-off. The *nanmu* coffin would only rot in the ground. And how much would seven pearls and seven gold coins cost? Want to ruin the family? Why, in forty-nine days our relatives and friends would eat you out of house and home! I can't bear you feeding them at *my* expense. Bah, get away, scram! Nothing doing."

After snubbing his eldest son he asked the second:

"How would *you* handle things?"

The second son thought his brother had overdone it.

"Don't worry, sir," he said. "My brother wanted more than we can afford, because we still have to live! We'll give you a fir-board coffin with no pearls inside, just seven gold coins. And there's no need for a gold bed-sheet and a silvery quilt embroidered with charms. We'll mourn for twenty-one days, with masses said every three days, not every day."

"No, that's still too much. Why, that would clean us out. No, no! Number Three! How would *you* handle it?"

His third son was clever and understood his father. He thought: I'll make the old fellow pop off with rage, then we can take our time arranging his funeral.

"What did you ask, sir?"

"How would you handle it?"

"I agree with you, my brothers were quite wrong. They don't know how to manage. The money you've worked so hard all your life to save, what a shame it would be if they squandered it like that! Besides, if we mourned for twenty-one days we'd have to feed all our relatives and friends. That would never do. I have a plan to set your mind at rest. We won't spend a cent on your funeral — we'll make some money instead!"

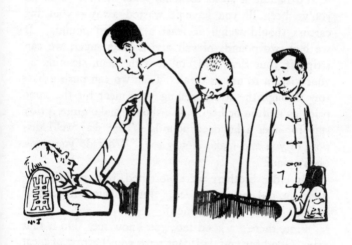

"... But push your barrow of meat to the south of our gate. Be sure not to take it north."

"The families to the north like to buy on credit."

The miser had never imagined that money could be made out of a dead man.

"How will you do that, eh? Tell me, There's a good lad. I want to hear how you would handle the business."

"I'd handle it so as to make some money. Though you've been ill you haven't wasted away — your big carcass should weigh at least a hundred pounds. If we buy two pounds of salt and a little sugar, we can strip off your flesh and boil it with them, cleaning up your viscera to use as offal. Then we can push a barrow through the street, selling your meat for the same price as mutton or beef. We should make quite a tidy sum for over a hundred pounds. That way we'd dispose of you and make money too. What do you think of my plan?"

His elder brothers were horrified, but to their surprise the old man approved. Just imagine, instead of losing his temper he beamed!

"Fine, there's a good lad, you know me. Do it that way. Good for you, lad! But push your barrow of meat to the south of our gate. Be sure not to take it north."

"Why not north?"

"The families to the north like to buy on credit."

He thought of everything!

(*Told by Zhang Shouchen*)

The Stupid Magistrate

IN the old days there was a saying: Men in the same line are bound to be enemies. Those who believed this lost out or landed themselves in trouble. When people in the same walk of life gunned for each other, even Buddhist monks and Taoist priests fell out. There are plenty of old stories about their squabbles and how their canons contradicted each other.

When someone died his family would set up canopies and ask Buddhist monks to recite sutras to release his soul from purgatory and urge it to go west, to the Western Paradise.

But a Taoist priest would urge the spirit to go east, to the realm of the sun.

A nun would call upon it to go south, to where Guanyin had her abode.

As for a lama, he would direct it north.

There are no spirits, of course. If there were, that would really be troublesome. Why? Well, how would a spirit know where to go with Buddhists, Taoists, nuns and lamas chanting different directions to it at the same time? Which of them should it listen to? Not knowing what to do, it could only circle round. Most likely those whirlwinds you see in the street are caused by such incantations. No, what a ridiculous notion!

Once something ludicrous happened. There was a monk roaming the country, begging for alms. One day in a teahouse he met an old Taoist priest, and while sipping their tea the two of them started chatting. Each boasted about himself and rather looked down on the other, and they fell to discussing their canons and beliefs.

The Taoist said, "It's best to be a Taoist, with a dignified get-up like mine. Listen to a verse I've made:

Blue robe and Taoist hat,
What sanctity!
A whisk in hand
He seems a deity."

The Buddhist said, "You're no deity. Deities don't look like you, they look like me. I've made a verse too.

He does good works,
Abstains from meat and wine,
Chants sutras all day long
Like an arhat divine.

As for you:

Long hair gets in your way,
You dress up every day.
Are you a woman or a man?
A disgusting sight, I say!"

This put the Taoist's back up. He retorted:

"With that patchwork cape of yours
And head shaved like a felon,
If your ears were cut off
You'd look like a watermelon."

That enraged the monk. So both of them lost their tempers and came to blows. In those bad old days the strangest things could happen. The Buddhist grabbed hold of the Taoist's hair and boxed him on the ears a dozen times. The Taoist tried to grab hold of the Buddhist, but this was hard because had no hair. Finally he grabbed his ears, yanked up his head and bit a hunk off his nose! That was the limit! The monk's face was streaming with blood. Everybody in the tea-house had crowded round to watch.

"What's the world coming to!" said one.

"Men in holy orders too!" another exclaimed. "If they carry on like this, what should we laymen do!"

Just then a bailiff came in and found them fighting, one with his nose bitten. Bloodshed made it a criminal case which couldn't be patched up in private but must be taken to court. So he hauled both the Buddhist and Taoist to the yamen. It so happened that the magistrate had got his post through bribery, and he hadn't been long in office or tried many cases. He had bungled every one. He was not only stupid but hen-pecked.

Hearing that there was a case to try, the magistrate held court. The yamen attendants raised an intimidating shout as he took his seat, flanked by his runners. He saw a Buddhist and a Taoist kneeling before him. The Buddhist's face was bloody. The magistrate asked him. "Why have you come to court?"

The monk said, "He bit my nose."

The magistrate asked the Taoist, "Why did you bite him?"

"I didn't, Your Honour," lied the Taoist. "He bit it himself."

The magistrate said, "You bit your own nose, monk, so why accuse someone else?"

That made the monk mad — how could he have bitten his own nose? He blurted out, "Your Honour, I couldn't reach it."

The magistrate thought: That makes sense. He told the Taoist, "He couldn't reach it."

The Taoist said, "He stood on a stool to bite it."

That convinced the magistrate. He bellowed, "You bold wretch of a monk, you stood on a stool to bite off your nose so as to put the blame on an innocent man. Here, give him a good beating — forty strokes!"

Poor monk! His nose was bitten off and after being beaten he was thrown into the lock-up, while a runner took the Taoist off to find someone to stand surety for him, then released him. And so in this offhand way the trial ended.

When the magistrate went back to his room his wife asked, "What was the case today that you settled so quickly?"

He told her, "It was a squabble between a priest and a monk. The rascally monk had bitten off his nose, but he wouldn't admit it and accused the Taoist of doing it. I gave him forty strokes and jailed him, and released the Taoist on bail. Not a bad day's work was it, madam?"

His wife knew he had muffed it again. She said, "No one, however clever, could reach his nose to bite it, sir."

"That's what I said," he answered. "But the Taoist told me he'd stood on a stool. You see, madam, by standing higher up he could reach it."

"However high you stand, you can't bite your own nose," she retorted. "Suppose I fetch a stool and you try for yourself?"

As the magistrate was rather afraid of his wife, he did as she suggested. He opened his mouth wide, but

"You bold wretch of a monk, you stood on the stool to bite off your nose so as to put the blame on an innocent man. Here, give him a good beating — forty strokes!"

couldn't bite his nose. Not understanding why, he asked,
"Isn't this stool too low, madam?"

"Very well," she said, "go up on the roof and see."

The magistrate at once went into the yard and
climbed up a ladder to the roof. When he had stood
there for a long time it dawned on him why he couldn't
bite his own nose.

His wife, both pleased and exasperated, said, "Come
down quick, and hurry up and get that Taoist arrested.
You must try the case again, and give him a good beating to make it up to the monk. Otherwise the people
here will hold it against you, and you may even be dis-
missed from your post. I'm afraid, though, you may
botch the business again. How can we avoid that?
Got it! I'll hide behind you in court and signal to you,
so that you'll know what to do. What do you say?"

The magistrate was delighted.

"Right you are!" At once he had the Taoist brought
back and took his seat in the court, his wife squatting
behind him, attendants ranged on both sides. The
Taoist knelt before him thinking: This time I'm for it.

The magistrate pounded his desk and demanded,
"Old Taoist, who bit the monk's nose?"

"Didn't you ask me before? He did it himself."

"That's wrong — how could he reach it?"

"Didn't he stand on a stool?"

"Rubbish. I climbed up the roof and still couldn't
reach it."

His wife thought: Why tell him that, you fool! She
twitched the magistrate's gown and put out four fingers,
meaning that the Taoist should be given forty strokes.

The magistrate seeing this said, "Give the Taoist four
strokes."

The Taoist thought: How kind-hearted he is, just giving me four strokes after all this. He lay face down to be beaten.

The wife thought: Botheration! I meant forty strokes, not four. Well, if he takes one finger for one stroke, five fingers for five strokes, if I turn my hand that will make ten strokes. Right. She tweaked the magistrate's gown again, stretched out five fingers and turned her hand over four times to make forty strokes.

When the magistrate saw this he ordered, "Turn the Taoist over to beat him."

This annoyed the Taoist. Who ever heard of beating a man lying on his back? This magistrate was a real fool. The attendants were shocked too, but they had to obey orders, so they lugged the Taoist by the legs and turned him over.

The magistrate's wife waved her hand to make him stop. What did that waving mean, he wondered? Ah, he knew. "Rub the Taoist's belly," he said.

The Taoist thought: I haven't got stomach-ache, so why rub my belly?

The magistrate's wife ground her teeth with rage. What did that mean, he wondered? Ah! He gave the order:

"Bite off the Taoist's nose."

Sweating and frantic, his wife ground her teeth, waved her hand and pointed at herself to signal: That's not what I meant. The magistrate was completely foxed. He said, "No, don't you bite it, let my wife bite it off."

(*Told by Zhang Yongxi*)

A Thief Talks

DO thieves talk? Would a thief climb on to a roof to wait for the people below to fall asleep, then lose patience and ask, "Why don't you turn in? Once you're asleep I can rob you!" No thief would do that.

There were plenty of thieves in the old days, not nowadays. Even so, you should shut your windows and door at night; otherwise, if you lose anything, don't expect me to take the responsibility. "Zhang Shouchen says there are no thieves, but I've lost something!" Well, that's nothing to do with me. Anyway, take care. Take care when? On wet or windy days, and especially before you go to bed. When the rain pelts down you say, "Listen to that downpour! Well, it cools things off — let's turn in early to sleep." In hot weather a cool spell helps you to sleep soundly. You wake to find yourself cleaned out — so watch out when it rains.

When the wind howls and someone thuds from the roof to the ground, the people indoors wonder: Has the high wind blown something down? But they don't go out — so the next day they find things missing!

"When lights are on the household's up" and "It's cowards who cough." What do these sayings mean? If someone indoors hears a noise outside and coughs, the thief won't go away. He knows that fellow's a coward. He's coughing to tell the thief, "Don't raise a rumpus. I'm nervous and I'm going to sleep; you can help yourself to anything you like." So he wakes to find everything gone!

If you hear movements outside and put on the light, you've had it! You're in the light, he's in the dark. He can see who you are, how many of you there are, what precautions you've taken against robbery. So here's my advice, if you hear movements outside: Stop talking and switch off the light, then the thief will skedaddle — he knows you're out to catch him!

Thieves don't generally talk, only on special occasions. One year we had a robbery in my place. You ask, "You had a robbery?" Well, that was under the Japanese occupation when the flour in the shops was mixed with dirt. You want to know what was stolen? In those days things were very different. Look at the way we live now. Take me for example. You can see I've plenty of flesh on my bones because I eat well and sleep soundly. I can come on stage wearing anything I like, that's why I'm wearing this tunic-suit. I pass muster anywhere in it, even on formal occasions. It wouldn't have done in the old days. If I'd worn this then on the stage, the audience would have booed me. You had to keep up appearances. In show business to do that we ran into debt. In summer we had to wear silk and satin gowns. Why? Two performances and you were drenched with sweat — you looked a sight! You needed at least two gowns to keep spruce and smart. In winter you had to have a fur jacket, an overcoat and an otter-skin cap. People seeing you couldn't tell that you were worried stiff about your debts! Why were clothes so important? They served many purposes. In the street they were casual clothes, at parties they were formal wear, on the stage they were costumes, in bed they were quilts, when you died they were shrouds — the same set of clothes. It was all I had. We had nothing else except for a mat on the *kang*.

That thief marked me out. He had his eye on me. "Zhang Shouchen must be rich with that fur jacket of his and an overcoat and otter-skin cap." He didn't know that we lived in one room without a stick of furniture, only a mat on the *kang*, not even a quilt! I covered myself with my clothes; my wife with her padded trousers, padded jacket and padded gown. We had no pillows. We both made do with one of my shoes. The wife had to keep hers on. Why? Her socks were worn through! That's how hard up we were.

Then a thief came. How did I know? We lived in a north room with the *kang* by the wall. I slept facing the door, with my cap on, its strings tied to keep out the cold. In the early hours I felt a draught on my head and opened my eyes. I saw someone creeping in, then closing the door. I knew it was a thief, but I didn't call out. Why not? If I'd startled him, he might have slashed me with the knife in his hand. Anyway I had nothing to lose; after groping around he could go and leave me in peace. I watched him grope around. He felt my clothes but couldn't tug them off. He didn't pull my cap off either for fear of waking me — though actually I was awake. And my shoes were under our heads. Apart from my wife and me, there was nothing on the *kang* but a mat. He went on groping. I thought: Why don't you leave? Clear off and let me sleep! Finally he groped his way to the southwest corner, and that gave me a fright. Why? That was where we kept our rice, over forty pounds of rice there in a vat. Under the Japs you couldn't buy rice, but

I just told her calmly, "Go to sleep, there's no thief." But then the thief butted in:

"No thief? If there's no thief, who's taken my jacket?"

I'd got a friend to get me this forty-odd pounds. Still, I knew he couldn't lug that vat on to the roof because with the rice it weighed over a hundred pounds, it was too heavy. Besides if he took it in the street he'd be arrested. Most thieves are superstitious, they won't go away empty-handed but must take a little something to bring themselves luck. All right, just take a handful to boil yourself some gruel, not enough for a bowl of rice. Why should I offend you? Just forget about me!

I watched him feel the vat, which had a lid on it made of sorghum stalks. He put the lid on the ground and fingered the rice. I thought: Why not take a bit? He stood there with his hands on his hips, thinking. Thieves are real devils. He hit on a way to fleece me. He took off his padded jacket and spread it on the ground before picking up the vat. I caught on. I thought: You rascal, you can't do that to me! He was going to empty the vat on to his jacket, leaving me at most a few ounces at the bottom. Well, I can't let you get away with that. When he turned to get the vat, I reached out for the collar of his jacket, pulled it on to the *kang* and lay on it. I gloated: Fine, an extra mattress for me. Let's see what you do now.

He didn't know. He picked up that vat and poured out the rice by my head. I chuckled to myself: You can't take that away, my lad! I shall just have to wash it clean before eating it. He put the empty vat back in the corner, then groped for his jacket to bundle it up and make off. When he couldn't find it that puzzled him. Did I empty out the rice in the wrong place? He scrabbled in the rice and felt the ground. He wondered: Where can I have put it?

"Eh?" he exclaimed. Couldn't find it anywhere. "Hell!"

His "Eh?" and "Hell!" were so loud that he woke my wife. She's easily scared, she kicked me. "Get up! Get up quick. There's a thief!"

I just told her calmly, "Go to sleep, there s no thief." But then the thief butted in:

"No thief? If there's no thief, who's taken my jacket?"

(Told by Zhang Shouchen)

Three Short-Sighted Brothers

WHAT'S the title of this item? *Three Short-Sighted Brothers.* The three of them were my uncles, all short-sighted. First Uncle couldn't see a thing in the morning; Second Uncle would bump right into a camel at noon; and Third Uncle was as blind as a bat in the evening.

Ha, those three uncles of mine, they kept making fools of themselves. When I was a kid First Uncle set off for Nanding outside the Yongding Gate to go to the temple fair held from the first to the fifteenth of the fifth month. Halfway there he decided to ask how much farther he had to go. He saw a man standing west of the road. Actually it wasn't a man. What was it then? A stone statue in a graveyard — a stone man and a stone horse! First Uncle asked this statue the way:

"Excuse me, sir, how far is it to Nanding?"

He repeated his question five times, but how could a statue talk? It just stood there.

"Hey! Are you deaf?"

A crow had perched on the statue's head. First Uncle waved his hand.

"Hey! You deaf?"

The crow flapped off. First Uncle chuckled, "Ha, you pig-headed fellow, refusing to tell me the way. Now your hat's blown off and I shan't tell you either."

See how his short-sightedness had held him up. That was First Uncle.

Second Uncle? He made a fool of himself too. One day in the street he met an old lady who had just bought a goose. What for? It was the rule in Beijing that when you arranged a marriage for your son, after his betrothal you had to send a goose to the girl's family. The old lady had this big white goose under her arm. Second Uncle saw how white it was, but couldn't make it out clearly.

"Not bad, that cotton wool! How much a pound?"

Cotton wool! The old lady thought he was talking to someone else who had bought cotton wool, so she paid no attention. Second Uncle stepped forward to feel it, asking again, "How much a pound is this cotton wool, old lady?"

He stroked the goose's plumage, slick and slippery.

"Oh, my mistake, it's lard."

He took it for lard!

"How much is this lard a pound?"

He reached down and caught hold of the goose's long neck.

"Why, here's a lotus root."

A lotus root! He tightened his grip. The goose honked and he let go.

"No, it's a horn!"

He got it wrong each time.

As for Third Uncle, he was invited one evening to an opera. It was summer, and when he started home it had just rained. A patch of cinders had been washed very clean, and a needle was sticking out of it, pointing upwards. Its glitter in the lamplight made his palm itch.

"A diamond, aha! This is worth money!"

He stepped over to pick it up, but pricked himself.
"Dammit, a scorpion! A scorpion!"

Under the street lamp he saw a sticky drop of blood
on his finger.

"Why, this isn't a scorpion, it's a lizard. Lizard!" he
said.

He rubbed it and bloodied his hand.

"Bah, a bedbug!"

Wrong every time!

These three uncles lived separately in three different
courtyards which opened on to two streets. First Uncle
and Second Uncle had houses on the front street, Third
Uncle on the back street. In summer they'd get together in First Uncle's courtyard, brew some tea and
sit in the shade to chat. Somehow the conversation
always came round to their eyesight. Why was that?
Anyone with a physical defect always tries to cover it
up, to make out that in this respect he's better than
other people. One day First Uncle lolled back in a
deck-chair.

"Well, Two and Three," he said. "My sight's improved so much recently that when a mosquito flies past
I can see whether it's a male or a female."

Second Uncle looked at him scornfully.

"Come off it. Last time you went out you bumped
into a steamroller. If you can't even see a steamroller,
how can you see mosquitoes?"

"My sight's better at night. The later it is, the more
clearly I can see."

Third Uncle said, "Quit squabbling, One and Two.
Stop boasting about your eyesight. You know that the
God of War's Temple outside this alley. Tomorrow

Three Short-Sighted Brothers 83

it's going to have a tablet put up. Let's go and have
a look at the inscription, and make a bet on it. Which-
ever of us sees it most distinctly will be treated to a
meal by the other two. What do you say to that,
brothers?"

First Uncle and Second Uncle said, "'Fine. We'll go
and see the tablet tomorrow."

At about midnight a cool wind sprang up, and Second and Third Uncle both went home to bed.

First Uncle lay on his *kang* but couldn't sleep. "This
won't do. When we look at the tablet tomorrow they'll
see it more clearly than I can. I don't mind treating
them to a meal, but I don't want them to say my eyesight's no good." Still, he had agreed to the bet, so what
could he do? At last he had an idea. "The monk in
the God of War's Temple must know what's on the
tablet, I'll go and ask him. I'll feel safer when I know
the inscription!" He got up, went to the temple and
knocked on the gate.

"Monk! Monk!"

The monk came out. So promptly? Well, at midnight he always got up to burn incense, so as soon as
he heard knocking he opened the gate.

"Who is it?"

He looked out.

"Oh, Master Zhang, please come in."

"No, thank you, I've come to trouble you. . . ."

"What can I do for you?"

"I hear you're putting up a tablet for the God of War
tomorrow."

"That's right. Donated by one of our patrons."

"Can you tell me the inscription on the tablet?"

The monk of course knew it.   He said, "It's 'Loyalty Everlasting'."

"Ha, 'Loyalty Everlasting!' Good. . . . Many thanks."

Having found this out he went off.   The puzzled monk closed the gate and went back to bed.

Then Second Uncle arrived.   Like First Uncle he was afraid he wouldn't be able to make out the inscription but would have to treat his brothers, who would make fun of him.   He left the alley just as First Uncle turned into it, but neither saw the other — that's how good their eyesight was! He knocked at the gate.

"Hey there, monk!"

The monk came out and saw it was Second Master Zhang.

"Please come in and sit down," he said.

"No, thanks. You're putting up a tablet tomorrow?"

"That's right, to the God of War."

"What inscription?"

"Loyalty Everlasting."

Second Uncle had more foresight than First Uncle.

"What colour is the tablet?"

"Blue with gold characters."

"So, blue with gold characters. Fine. . . . See you tomorrow."

Second Uncle left and the monk went back to bed, but then along came Third Uncle.   He couldn't sleep either for worrying. He'd come by the back street.

"Monk, monk!"

The monk said:

"No sleep for me tonight!"

He came out and saw Third Master Zhang.

"Oh, Third Master Zhang, come on in."

"No, thanks.   Tomorrow. . . ."

"We're hanging up a tablet to the God of War. The inscription 'Loyalty Everlasting' is in gold characters on a blue ground."

Third Uncle, being the youngest, was smarter than his brothers.

"Anything else written above or below?"

"Yes."

"What's written above?"

"The date in red. Down below is 'respectfully presented by a true believer', 'presented' is in red, the rest in gold."

"I see. Thank you very much."

He went off, and at last the monk could sleep.

First Uncle got up early the next morning. He gargled and was brushing his teeth when his two brothers arrived.

"Elder Brother!"

"Oh, Two, Three, come in, have a drink of water."

"Why drink water? We can drink when we get back. Let's go and see the tablet."

"Right you are."

The toothbrush was put down, and the three of them set off hand in hand to the temple. As soon as they were out of the alley, First Uncle pointed at the temple gate.

"Right, stay put, don't go any closer. Go any closer and anybody can see it. Ha! Now we'll test our eyesight. Look!"

In fact they were still some distance from the temple.

"A fine tablet, 'Loyalty Everlasting'. 'Loyalty Everlasting'."

First Uncle was illiterate, but now he tried to show off, "See how well the last character's written."

In fact he didn't know the first thing about calligraphy.

Second Uncle said, "Elder Brother, your sight's certainly improved. You can see 'Loyalty Everlasting' quite clearly. But those big characters aren't hard to make out. Can you see what colour they are, the characters and the tablet?"

That floored First Uncle. He thought, "Confound it, I forgot to ask that last night."

Second Uncle said, "Can't make it out, eh? The tablet's blue, the characters are gold. Ha, I can see more clearly!"

Third Uncle said, "Second Brother's sight is better than Elder Brother's. But those big characters 'Loyalty Everlasting are easy to see. And gold characters on a blue ground are so clear in the sunlight, you'd have to have very poor eyesight not to see them. Can you read what's written above and underneath?"

Second Uncle was floored, he hadn't asked. Third Uncle said, "You can't, eh, either of you? I'll read it out to you. Above is written the date in red. Below is 'respectfully presented by a true believer', 'presented' in red, the other words in gold. Well, how about it? Not a word missing! My eyesight is the best. Which of you is going to treat me?"

First Uncle said, "Well, Three doesn't have to pay. But I was the first to see 'Loyalty Everlasting', so I don't have to pay either. Two must stand treat."

Second Uncle said, "That's not fair. I made out the colour, which is more than you did. You must stand treat. Or suppose you pay four fifths, I pay one fifth, and Three nothing."

"No, I'm not paying."

The monk laughed....
"You came too early. I haven't hung up the tablet yet!"

They were shouting now, about to come to blows. Then the monk came out.

"Ha, you gentlemen are up early."

"Oh, good, here is the monk."

They tugged him over.

"Your tablet is to the God of War, right?"

"That's right."

First Uncle said, " 'Loyalty Everlasting', isn't it?"

The monk said, "Right."

Second Uncle asked, "Gold characters on blue, eh?"

The monk said, "Quite right."

Third Uncle said, "And this is what's written above and underneath, right?"

The monk said, "You've got it all right."

"Good, we made a bet on this, the losers to stand the winner a treat. You come and join us, monk. You say who's won and who's lost. We'll take your word for it."

The monk laughed.

"I say you three brothers must treat me, because you all lost. I'm the only winner! You three will have to treat me to a meal."

"How can *you* be the winner?"

"You came too early. I haven't hung up the tablet yet!"

(Told by Zhang Shouchen)

The Fearful Footman

IN the Qing Dynasty, in Dumb Alley at the east end of Beijing there lived an official named Zeng. The youngest of nine brothers he was known as Ninth Master Zeng. Ninth Master was a stickler for keeping up appearances and living in great style. He made strict rules for his servants and would swear at them or beat them if they didn't behave exactly to his liking; so all the footmen in Beijing knew what a terror he was and wouldn't work for him at any price. Ninth Zeng was in a fix. He was used to being waited on by two footmen whenever he went out, entertained visitors or amused himself; but now he was left high and dry!

One day, the thirteenth of April, he suddenly remembered that on the twentieth there would be a wedding in the house of his sworn brother Third Master Men, who lived in Tan Jar Alley at the far west end of Beijing. He would have to go to offer congratulations. But he had no footmen. Could he get his groom to carry in his presents for him? That would make people split their sides laughing! In desperation he hit on a plan. Zhao Er, who had looked after his family's graveyard in the country, had a son. If Ninth Master sent for him he would have to come.

Zhao Er's son, Number Three, was seventeen or eighteen, an honest, close-mouthed youngster. Because he looked so honest Ninth Master called him Dumb Num-

ber Three. In fact Number Three was not really dumb
— he had good sense. His father had died worn out
by minding Ninth Master's graveyard and tilling his
land. Then Ninth Master tried to trick Number Three,
telling him:

"Your dad's dead, Number Three, so I'll let you
mind my graveyard and till my fields. After the harvest
you needn't pay me rent, just give me grain."

"How much grain, Ninth Master?"

"All the crop above ground. You can keep what's
underground."

"All right." Number Three nodded.

After the harvest he carted his crop to Ninth Master.
When Ninth Zeng saw it he flared up. Number Three
had grown nothing but yams, and had kept the yams
for himself, giving the landlord the vines. But angry as
he was, Ninth Master couldn't object as he had asked
for what grew above the ground. Accepting the vines
he said:

"Next year we'll switch. I'll take what's underground,
you keep what's above ground."

"Very well," said Number Three.

The next autumn he brought two more cartloads of
his produce from underground. When Ninth Master
saw it he nearly had a fit. This time Number Three
had grown sorghum and brought him two cartloads of
the roots. Before Number Three left he told him:

"Next year bring me the tips from the bottom and
top. You can keep the middle part."

Number Three agreed to this. The next year he grew
maize and delivered Ninth Zeng two cartloads of tassels
and roots. Ninth Master raised a great row; but his

wife Ninth Mistress reasoned, "Never mind, he's a fool, so it's no use your losing your temper with him."

Ninth Master said, "He's no fool, but he's made a fool of me!"

Now Ninth Master had to go to a wedding feast but had no footmen. He suddenly thought of Number Three. But when he consulted his wife she said, "How can you take such a fool along with you?"

"He may look a fool," said Ninth Zeng. "But he's really smart. I can tell him what to do. And I shan't have to pay him, as he minds our family graveyard." The thought of saving money made his wife agree. So Number Three was sent for.

Number Three came to the Zengs' mansion. After greeting Ninth Master and Ninth Mistress he stood there waiting for orders.

Ninth Master Zeng said, "I've sent for you to promote you to be a footman. If you show good sense, later on I'll get you a job in the yamen that's better than farming."

"Right," said Number Three.

Ninth Mistress said, "Mind you wait on the master well and work hard. Don't be such a dolt. All right, you can go now."

So Number Three stayed there. Nothing happened that night. The next day Ninth Master got up early to wash and dress. He wore an official robe and belt, and over this a jacket designed with eight red and black dragons. He put on his black brocade boots and his tasselled hat complete with button and feather. Then he took his beads and put on his outer jacket embroidered with golden unicorns. Having placed his card and list of gifts in the casket of presents, he brought out the pipe which he used when paying visits. The stem of this pipe was of ebony, the bowl of white brass, the mouthpiece of green jadeite, so that when he puffed at it half his face turned green. He thought this pipe too precious to use at home, but always took it out when paying visits. Now he hadn't been out for a month for lack of footmen. Today when he tried the pipe it seemed to be blocked. He told Number Three:

"Number Three, take this pipe and clean it out for me."

Number Three took the pipe and asked, "How to clean it, sir?"

"There's a wire hanging on the wall outside the kitchen. Use that."

Number Three went to the kitchen, removed the mouthpiece and bowl of the pipe and laid them on the window-sill. Instead of looking for the wire to clean the stem of the pipe he picked up a poker. But try as he might he couldn't stick this in. His eye fell on a hammer for breaking up coal on the steps, and he used this to hammer the poker into the pipe stem. That was more like it. Crack! The pipe split in two. Number Three jumped in fright. "That's torn it!" As he stood there wondering what to do, Ninth Master shouted to him from the study. He was frantic. He saw hanging over the window a steelyard about the same length and thickness as the pipe. He snatched it down, took off its metal weight, hook and string, and fixed on the mouthpiece and bowl, so that it looked like a pipe with steelyard markings on it. He took it back to the study.

"Why were you so slow?" swore Ninth Master. "Hurry up and put it in my tobacco pouch. You're to carry that and the casket of presents. Come on!"

His groom had the cart ready waiting outside. He at once put a stool beside it for the master to mount. First Ninth Zeng got his left knee on the cart and leaned forward, bending his head so as not to knock off his feather. Then he sat down hunched up in the cart.

Number Three asked from below, "Where am I to sit, sir?"

Ninth Master was already angry with him for taking so long to clean his pipe, yet there he was asking this idiotic question. "There's no seat for you," he snapped. "You run behind!"

It's a good fifteen *li* from the east end of Beijing to the west, making a detour round the Forbidden City. By the time Number Three reached the home of Third Master Men he was too tired to speak, puffing and panting. Ninth Zeng took him in to greet Third Master Men and offer congratulations, then the host took Ninth Zeng to the hall to drink tea. The hall was packed with guests, all of whom stood up to raise clasped hands in greeting, calling him Ninth Elder Brother or Ninth Younger Brother. He was given the seat of honour and they started chatting. Number Three neither filled his pipe nor poured tea, just stood panting behind his master. The other guests were puzzled. They thought: Ninth Master Zeng usually brings a few well-trained footmen to wait on him. Why has he just brought such a dolt today? Someone poured out a bowl of tea and offered it to him.

"Have some tea, Ninth Master."

Seeing that it was someone else's footman, Ninth Zeng inclined his head and thanked him politely. But it wouldn't have been correct to drink the tea at once. Meantime Number Three, hot and thirsty after running, was longing for a drink. Seeing that Ninth Master hadn't drunk his bowl, he reached out for it saying:

"If you're not drinking, sir, I will." With that he gulped down the tea.

"Put that down!" ordered Ninth Master.

"All right, I'll put it down."

When Ninth Master saw the empty bowl he was furious, but he couldn't make a scene in front of his host. He fumed:

"Here! Fill my pipe!"

"Right!" said Number Three.

He produced the pipe, filled the bowl with tobacco and set the mouthpiece to Ninth Master's lips, then lit a spill to light the tobacco. Ninth Master, talking to the other guests, puffed at the pipe, but no matter how hard he puffed no smoke came out.

"Light it!" he ordered Number Three.

"I've been holding this spill to the bowl all this time!"

Ninth Master's lips ached from puffing, yet still no smoke had come out.

"Didn't you clean this pipe, Number Three?" he asked.

"I did!"

"Well then why can't I get it to draw? What's wrong with it?"

Ninth Master looked at the pipe and so did the other guests. Ha! What were all those steelyard markings on the stem?

"What's this, Number Three?"

"A steelyard."

That set the whole company laughing. Ninth Master turned purple with rage and embarrassment.

"Clear off! Go back!" he roared.

. . . Ha! What were all those steelyard markings on the stem?

"What's this, Number Three?"

"A steelyard."

"All right, I'll go back."

Number Three went out of the gate to find the groom. "Come on," he said. "The master wants me to go back by cart."

The groom had only just unhitched the mule. When he heard this he thought, "Fine, I can go home and sleep."

He harnessed the mule, made Number Three sit in the cart, and with a flourish of his whip drove off.

Ninth Zeng enjoyed himself all day in Third Master Men's house. After dinner he took his leave and his host saw him to the inner gate. There Ninth Zeng stopped him, saying, "Third Brother, don't come any farther." Third Master Men raised his clasped hands in salute, then went back to the hall to see to his other guests. Once out of the gate Ninth Zeng looked around. There were plenty of carts and mules, but he couldn't see his. Standing on the steps he shouted:

"Where is my cart?"

Someone told him, "Ninth Master, it's gone.'

"What! Who told him to go back?"

"That steward of yours went back in it."

Ninth Zeng rolled his eyes, livid. But there was no help for it — he would have to walk back. There were no trams or taxis in those days. That walk nearly did him in. Had he been wearing his everyday clothes he could have stopped to rest when he was tired. But he was in his official robes and jacket, his official boots, feathered hat and beads — in that get-up he had to walk with measured steps. He couldn't stop to rest, while to hurry would have finished him off. Step by step he had to stagger the whole way home — it was really killing. By the time he reached his gate, sagging and stooped, he could only shuffle forward inch by inch. Ninth Mistress, watching by the window, saw him waddle in like a duck. She hurried out.

"Why, sir! What's happened?"

"Confound it!" he swore. "I'll tell you inside."

Ninth Mistress helped him in and, huffing and puffing, he told her all that happened, then stuck out his feet.

"Look, wife. My feet are all over blisters!"

She looked and saw that his feet were a mass of big blisters. So she called the maid-servant. "Amah Zhang, go and fetch Number Three."

Number Three was asleep in bed. Amah Zhang woke him up and sent him to see the master. At sight of him, Ninth Zeng's eyes flashed fire and he leapt up to beat him. But when he heaved himself off the *kang* the soles of his feet hurt like hell — he couldn't walk. His wife quickly held him up and told Number Three, "You idiot, what right had you to come back in the master's cart? See, by walking back he's blistered both his feet. I'm scared to prick blisters, so you must go and fetch a chiropodist for us."

"What's chiropodist?" Number Three asked.

"A man who pares toe-nails with a knife."

"Where can I find one?"

Ninth Zeng was now so mad that, ignoring the pain in his feet he jumped off the *kang* and kicked Number Three.

"Go and look, you wretch! Go out and find one!"

Number Three went off pouting. "All right, I'll look. Why kick me?"

You can find chiropodists in bath-houses or at temple fairs. But Number Three, being new to town, didn't know this. He searched the streets. When he reached Hademen he saw a smithy where two men were shoeing a horse. One of them was cutting the horse's hoof with a knife. Number Three thought: Ah, I've found a chiropodist. He went over and said:

"Hey! Come along to our place."

The blacksmiths thought he wanted them to go and shoe a horse.

"How many?" they asked.

"One," said Number Three. He left out the word "man".

"Is it skittish?" they asked. "If it kicks we'll take a curb to tie it up so that it can't kick."

"Yes, take one," said Number Three. "He likes to kick people. Gave me a kick, he did, just before I came."

At once the blacksmiths took a curb, knife, hammer, nails and horseshoes and followed Number Three to the Zeng mansion. At the front gate Number Three told them, "Come on in." When they reached the inner gate the two blacksmiths waited in the yard. Ninth Master, watching at the window, saw them and told his wife:

"See that — he's treating me like a horse!"

That same moment Number Three came in. "The chiropodists are here, sir. Shall I bring them in?"

By way of answer Ninth Zeng leapt off the *kang* and aimed two vicious kicks at him. Number Three ran out yelling:

"Chiropodists! Quick! Bring your curb to tie him up — he's kicking people again!"

(Told by Zhang Shouchen)

Melted Candlesticks

THIS happened to our neighbour — the oddest things keep happening to this neighbour! You want to know where I live? Don't ask. Just hear this tale for what it's worth.

Over forty years ago, our neighbours were a well-to-do family. They had big houses, land and fat bank accounts. This family was called Wolf. You say there's no such surname? So much the better, I won't risk meeting someone else with the same name. In this Wolf family lived an old husband and wife, their three sons and their daughter. The three sons married, and now the time was coming to marry the daughter off. The whole household got busy preparing sixty-four loads of dowry, eight camphor-wood chests, and two halls full of china. What china? In the old days they were particular to have teapots, bowls, whisk pots, everything made in the best kilns. In addition there was a set of pewterware: tea caddies, oil lamps, candlesticks. They put honey in the oil lamps to sweeten the bridal chamber! More than forty pounds of pewter, and all of it top quality — if tapped it rang like copper....

Less than two years after the daughter's marriage the old man died. Then his widow was up against it. Why? With the old man dead, who was in charge? All three brothers tried to run the show, and their wives bickered. They kept the kitchen stove lit the whole year round! Why was that? Cooking all the time. First Master liked noodles for breakfast, Second Master griddle-cakes, Third Master baked buns and fish; First Mistress rice, Second Mistress steamed rolls, and Third Mistress dumpling soup. How to satisfy everyone? After eating they sat indoors cursing, cursing their children or their cats if they'd no children. They gave their neighbours no peace. Day and night they squabbled. At first the neighbours tried to intervene, but later they paid no attention even if they came to blows. What could be done? The only thing was to split up.

They invited all their relatives and friends to a feast to divide up the property. Each son got some houses. If his share was worth less than his brothers' it was made up to him with money from the bank. What remained in the bank was split into three shares, as were all the movables down to the last chopstick, which they split into three. They even counted the coal-balls! Finally nothing was left but a copper coin. To whom should that go? Nobody could have it! Well? Buy a copper's worth of fried beans to share out, and if one was left over throw it into the street rather than let anyone have it! Hens, cats, dogs, all were divided; but what about mother? With whom should she live? None of them had thought about that. First Master would be staying in the old house. Second and Third would move out. So now that they had divided up the loot, they loaded their shares on to carts at the gate and took their leave.

"We're off now, kinsmen and friends, to move house."

Their sister was still young, in her early thirties, but she had a good head on her shoulders. She had sat there chuckling without a word, but now she asked, "Off now, Second and Third Brother?"

"You stay put, sister, we're not waiting for supper, we must go and settle in."

"Why be in such a hurry to leave when there's something not yet shared out?"

Her three brothers gaped in astonishment.

"What's that? What else is there, sister?"

"There's still mother! How will you share her between you? Not going to strangle her and divide her into three, are you? Or slice her up alive?"

"What an idea!"

Their relatives and friends pricked up their ears. The old lady hadn't raised this daughter for nothing! At first the three brothers were flummoxed. Then First Master said, "Sister's right, quite right. Who'd dare strangle her? Between us we should provide a pension for her; but after her death we'd still have to divide it up, and how troublesome that would be! Let's divide it up today to save trouble later. I know a way out. Thirty days in a month, mother can stay with each of us for ten days. Today's the first and she's here. On the eleventh Second Master will fetch her, on the twenty-first Third Master, and on the first of next month I'll bring her back. Fetch or take her in the same way, what d'you say to that?"

The guests approved, "That's the way."

Then everyone went home.

All went well the first day. The old lady had leftovers from the feast for her evening meal. The day after that First Master had to feed her. That was when her troubles started. You should have seen them! She got up and sat there, and her daughter-in-law — First Mistress — poured her tea while her son stood beside her.

"Sit down, son."

"Oh no, madam. I know how fond you are of me, but if I sat with you what would people think? They'd call me lacking in respect, haha, or say you're too soft with us.... I'd like to discuss something with you, if you're willing; if not, it can wait for another day."

The old lady asked, "What is it? Go ahead."

"Sure?"

"Of course. Why not?"

"All right. Do you want me to do well? Or beg for a living?"

The old lady said, "What a strange question! Whatever hurts my children hurts me. I want you all to do well, not to beg for a living!"

"I know, I know how fond you are of me. You want me to do well, and so do I; but it isn't easy. When we lived together my brothers were careful managers; now that we've split up each has to fend for himself. They both have ways and means, but I'm left stranded. I shall have to skimp and save, just eating cornflour. Why tell you this? I don't want to upset you! You'll only spend ten days a month here, so you shall have whatever you fancy to eat. We'll cook just enough for you; don't share it with the children. And never mind if we go hungry or just eat congee; you can have anything you fancy."

The old lady said, "What nonsense, that isn't right. Why cook special dishes for me? I hope you manage all right, but if you're short how can I eat you out of house and home? Not I! I don't eat much anyway, and

I'm not fussy. The ten days I'm here I'll eat whatever
you have. Cornflour is fine with me."

"All right, if you like cornflour, you shall have that
— whatever you like. Wife, prepare a meal!"

The scoundrel, he'd put these words in his mother's
mouth. His wife went off to cook the meal. Instead
of steaming some soft cornflour buns, she baked some
huge, half-burnt corn-cakes on a hot fire, without even
any pickles to go with them. Half the old lady's teeth
were missing; she couldn't chew those charred corn-
cakes, could only eat a third of the softer part. Was
she too choosy? No, most people over fifty are like
that: they need good nourishing food to satisfy them.
If food is too hard to swallow they have to go hungry.
What then? Pretend to be satisfied! She left the corn-
cakes, thinking: I'm still hungry, but never mind, they're
bound to have some gruel this evening. I can soak
these corn-cakes in gruel. That's where she was wrong:
that evening they served up the left-over corn-cakes!
Just toasted them which made them even harder.

So after a couple of bites, the old lady put her cake
down — she'd had enough! After supper First Master
took his two big sons out to have some snacks in restaurants outside, coming home when they were full. First
Mistress? She took the baby and her daughters to play
cards with some neighbours. Not hungry? She gave
the girls money to buy flat bread and braised pork sea-
soned with soysauce, and when they had filled themselves up they went home again. The corn-cakes were
kept for the old lady. By the sixth day more than
half were still left! The old lady realized she wouldn't
be able to finish them by the tenth. Go and stay with
Second Master! So off she went. Her eldest son and

daughter-in-law didn't ask where she was going, and she didn't tell them.

When the old lady reached Second Master's house, his first words to her were, "So it's you, ma! Weren't you to come on the eleventh? Why turn up today? You mean to stay half a month here? Why didn't you make this clear?"

She sat down panting, "Ai! Your brother baked a batch of corn-cakes, that's all I've had to eat the last five days. I'm too famished to go on this way!"

"So that's it. Well, at least he has corn-cakes, that's more than we do. Of course, now that you're here we'll have to feed you, can't let you go hungry. Since you won't eat good corn-cakes, suppose we make you corn-meal congee."

Cornmeal congee sounded good, easy on the teeth! Yes, that should slip down nicely! They used half a pound of cornmeal to make a big pan. After two days there was still half of it left; but the old lady was starving. She would go to her third son!

As soon as her third son saw her he cried, "Not dead yet, you? Why not die and be done with it? We'd put on white mourning for you! Are you trying to eat us up? You shouldn't be here till the twenty-first, and it's not yet the tenth. What are you playing at?"

She told him, "Your elder brother baked me a batch of corn-cakes which I ate for five days. Your second brother made me a pan of such watery congee, I could only drink half of it in two days. I'm simply famished."

"So that's it. They don't squander their money on you but on themselves, the swine! My share of money and property has all gone on paying debts. Can't owe people money, can I? They'd sue me! I've had to mortgage this house. We had nothing to eat yesterday. But now you've come how can we let you go hungry? We'll beg for some food for you. I've no money, have you any money, wife?"

"Not I."

"Ask the boys if they have any."

They found that the oldest boy had a copper on him.

"What can we buy for a copper? I know, buy your grandma some fried broad beans."

Fine! After baked corn-cakes and that watery congee, she was invited to break her teeth on hard beans! She managed to eat three and kept one in her mouth when she went to bed — it nearly choked her that night! The old lady decided her only hope was to appeal to her daughter. If that failed she would simply have to jump into the river!

Too weak to walk to her daughter's house, she hired a rickshaw and told the man to knock at the gate and call her grandson's pet name, saying his granny had come. At once her daughter came out, and discovered her mother at her last gasp! At sight of her daughter she wept! The young woman understood. She dried her mother's tears and paid off the rickshawman.

"Don't cry or people will laugh at us. Come on in." She and the rickshawman helped the old lady inside and sat her down. When the rickshawman left, the old lady wanted to speak, but her daughter covered her mouth.

"Don't give the neighbours this chance to laugh at us. I know just how you feel, know just what your three sons and daughters-in-law have been up to. Some daughters might be afraid to let you in, for fear you might die here. But I know there's nothing wrong with your health, you're just hungry! I can't let you eat your fill, though, because if you overeat on an empty stomach that could finish you off! Then my brothers would come to put the blame on me. So first let me cosset you for a couple of days."

The first day she made the old lady some arrowroot and fried-flour soup; the next day some soup with eggs; the third day some noodles and dumplings. After a week she had fish; after two weeks stewed meat! By the end of the month the old lady had recovered and was bursting with energy. She didn't want to leave, she wanted to stay there.

One night when her son-in-law had gone out and the children were asleep, mother and daughter sat chatting.

The daughter said, "I've a proposal, but you mustn't let it upset you. Sons and daughters should support the parents who brought them up; and sometimes a son-in-law takes care of his mother-in-law, but only when she has no sons of her own or they are badly off. Your three sons have jobs and earn money. Each owns houses and land and has over ten thousand in the bank. You know I love having you here; but there's always some friction between husband and wife, and if ever we were to quarrel and he had this handle against me, I'd never live it down! I've thought up a trick to play, and if you'll keep it a secret I guarantee your sons and daughters-in-law will lean over backwards to be filial to you! Their children will flock round to see which of them can be most dutiful. But don't let the cat out of the bag, or the trick won't work. Sons and daughters-in-law would treat you like dirt, the grandchildren would look through you — they'd leave you to beg in the street. And you mustn't come back here if you let out the secret."

By now the old lady was willing to take her daughter's word for anything. What trick were they going to play? I'll come to that presently. The old lady asked:

"Will it work?"

"It will!"

"All right. Whatever you say, daughter."

They set to work together. No lack of firewood at home, so first they lit the big stove in the kitchen and carried in all the pewterware in the daughter's dowry — forty pounds and more. This they melted down in a great cauldron. Then with the poker the daughter made some oblong as well as round hollows in the ground, into which she poured molten pewter. When this had cooled she removed it and poured in more, keeping this up half the night till their *kang* was piled with oblong bars and round ingots. Next she fetched over ten feet of white cloth to make a wrap-around pouch — this wide — in which she sewed the rows of pewter ingots. This done, she made her mother take off her gown and wrap this pouch round her waist. She sewed the whole thing up securely, and attached two cords to the bottom to fasten crosswise.

By the time the old lady was dressed again it was light; and her daughter served her some soya milk and refreshments. She then gave her ten silver dollars, and a dollar in small notes and coppers. Having put this in her pocket she called a rickshaw for her.

"Now go to your eldest son and do as we agreed. I haven't paid for the rickshaw. You can pay at the gate."

So the old lady went back to First Master's house, where her elder daughter-in-law was buying fish at the gate. She ignored her mother-in-law. But when the old lady fumbled for her fare, ha! two silver dollars clinked to the ground, and the rickshawman picked them up. "Here, you've dropped your money, old lady."

"Oh, how kind of you! There are good people in every trade. I didn't see, and someone else might have filched it. Thank you, thank you. . . . Thirty coppers fare. Here's twenty cents. Keep the change."

Twenty cents! In those days ten cents fetched more fifty coppers!

Her daughter-in-law was staggered to see how open-handed she was, scattering money right and left and not asking the rickshawman for any change.

As the rickshawman prepared to help the old lady off, her daughter-in-law hurried over.

"I'll help her. Where have you been, madam? I was going to fetch you! Let me help her down."

Holding the baby in one arm, she put the other round the old lady's waist. You ask: How did she know what the old lady had there? Just listen! As the old lady walked she propped up her pouch. You ask: Why? Over forty pounds — it was heavy! Seeing this First Mistress thought: She's got something there. With her free hand she groped and felt something hard.

"First Master! Madam's back!"

First Master hadn't heard her called "madam" since his father died. He jumped up on his stockinged feet.

"Oh, ma! Where have you been? I was meaning to fetch you. Ho!"

His wife told him, "Help her inside."

"Right." First Master put his hand under her arm while his wife let go, casting him a meaning glance and jerking her chin towards the old lady's waist. First Master, catching on, helped his mother indoors.

"Sit down, sit down." He poured her tea. "Where have you been? We wanted to fetch you back."

"Why should you fetch me, haven't I come myself? Why shouldn't I come home? I tell you, son, in this world men and women alike need sense to get by. When your dad was alive I kept my wits about me, and stowed away some savings in your sister's place. Now I've reclaimed them. Why? I'll tell you, it doesn't matter your feeding me cornflour; you couldn't help it if you'd no way of earning money! And cornflour is filling. When I went to your second brother's he could only give me congee; well, congee is grain too! My third son gave me fried broad beans, hoping I'd choke to death — wasn't that the limit! All right, I won't be a burden to anyone, I've brought my small savings along and I'll stay with whoever treats me decently. Now I've come to you, but I'm not going to live on you. . . . You can clear out any room you like for me, and I'll pay a fair rent for it. I'll hire a maid to wait on me and cook for the two of us; if the children like to eat with me I won't shoo them away, if they don't want to then I won't insist. Anyway I've enough to spend, and can die in peace not caring how much is left. Just clear me out a room! Find me a maid."

The eldest son, hearing this, slapped his cheeks hard four times.

"Ma, ma! Don't say such things! Thank goodness no friends or kinsmen are here, or what kind of a worm would they think me? I'd rather be stabbed with a knife! I was a scoundrel to make you angry, should kneel for you to beat me. Let's say no more about it! How can you possibly pay us rent? This whole house is yours and we belong to you, flesh and bone! Besides,

how can a maid wait on you as well as your daughter-
in-law? You were the one who said you wanted to eat
cornflour, we didn't know you didn't mean it! If you
don't like it, why ever didn't you say so? Here, stew
some pork for the mistress!"

So pork was stewed at once. When the old lady had
finished it, they took her out to an opera, hired a box!
After the opera they had a meal in a restaurant, then
went home while the sun was still high in the sky. By
now her *kang* was ready.

"Why not have a sleep, now, madam!"

"Why so early?"

"Turn in early to build up your strength! Early to
bed and early to rise, aha!"

They helped the old lady to the bed. Her daughter-
in-law took her cane from her, and the old lady sat on
the edge of the *kang*. Then her daughter-in-law offered
to undress her.

"Hey!" The old lady stood up and picked up her
cane. "That won't do, don't touch my clothes! I know
you mean well and only want to help. But I can't
undress. If you insist, I'll call the police! If you touch
my clothes I'll leave! I tell you, it's my life I have here,
so nobody's to touch it. Enough for me for the rest of
my days, and what happens to it when I'm gone I don't
care. Touch my clothes and I'll go away even without
a rickshaw."

First Master said, "All right, don't take on like that.
You can sleep in your clothes, mama, so much the better
— you won't catch cold."

That night husband and wife went seven times to
tuck in the old lady's quilt. You say: Tuck it in? Not
tuck it in but undo it. As the lights were out First

Master carried a torch. "Don't kick off your quilt or catch cold, madam! Tuck it up tight."

One tucking up the quilt, one pulling it back, they shone the torch on the old lady's waist and felt it carefully before covering her again and scuttling out. They whispered to each other, "All those long ones must be ten-ounce bars of gold, the short ones five-ounce bars; the round and square ones silver ingots. Looks as if there's more gold than silver!... We mustn't annoy her or run the risk of her leaving. Wake the children up except baby who's too small to understand, wake the big ones up! Go on!"

But the teenage boys refused to wake up — they had been on the go all day.

"They won't wake. What if they get up to mischief tomorrow and vex their grandmother? Tickle the soles of their feet."

When tickled the boys woke up. But they fell straight asleep again.

"Dammit, they're sleeping again."

They fetched cold water and spattered the boys' faces.

"Are your heads clear now?"

"Yes."

"If they're not, take a stroll in the yard in the cold wind, then come back."

"What for?"

"What for? I'll tell you. Starting from tomorrow, you must amuse your grandmother if she wants you; if she doesn't, make yourselves scarce. Tell her only what she likes to hear. If you annoy her so that she leaves for good, we'll tear you monkeys to pieces!"

"Right, we understand."

So that first night they gave the boys these instructions. The next day they gave the old lady whatever she asked for to eat.

She had been there only four days when somehow word of this reached Second Master. He came to sit in front of his mother weeping.

The old lady asked, "Who's upset you?"

"Nobody. If I'm not mean to anyone, no one's mean to me. But now everyone's saying that though I'm your son too, you stay here with my brother, not with me, and that looks bad! How can I make a good impression outside?"

He carried his mother off! But three days later, when First Master wanted her back she wasn't there any more. Where had she gone? Third Master had carried her off, and he had to fetch her from there.

To cut a long story short, these three sons gave their mother whatever she wanted to eat, then took her to see an opera or film and urged her to go to bed. But when they asked her to take off her clothes, she threatened to call the police. This went on for a whole two and a half years. Then the three brothers put their heads together.

First Master said, "Let's stop carrying her off, or people will laugh at us. It's all for that hoard she has wrapped round her waist, isn't it? Let's not do anything to make her angry, just let her have her way in everything. When she passes on, we'll share and share alike. But if anyone annoys her and she says he's not to get a share, we'll have to abide by that."

His two brothers agreed to this, and wherever she went they treated her more dutifully than ever. They and their wives were most filial, but all of them wished.... What did they wish? That she would hurry up and die and be done with it!

Far from dying, the old lady's health improved. How could that be when she was over seventy? In the first place she was pleased, what with her sons and daughters-in-law so filial, her grandsons and grand-daughters all flocking round her. In the second place, she could eat whatever she fancied. In the third place, carrying more than forty pounds of pewter about with her all the time had strengthened her!

So what happened? Well, old people have to take great care of their health. One evening in Second Master's house the old lady had indigestion and drank some warm water, so she had to get up several times in the night. This meant, she knew, that she wasn't long for this world. She couldn't go on keeping watch over her hoard; and if her sons and daughters-in-law were to discover that it was only pewter, she'd be thrown out to die in the street! She had previously agreed not to see her daughter. So now that her daughter hadn't come for a long time, she went out the next morning with her cane and gave one of the children in the street a dollar to fetch her.

The daughter arrived before ten and saw First Master lead in a western doctor, while Second and Third Master saw off two other physicians. What had happened? Second and Third Master had fetched two practicioners of Chinese medicine to make out prescriptions. Now the western doctor made out a prescription too. After he had left, Second Brother said:

"So you've come, sister. Shall we make up these

Chinese prescriptions or this western one? I'll see to it."

First Master said, "Wait, it's a good thing our sister's come, or we'd have had to send for her. The four of us must figure this out together. After all, even though we've split up, the same mother bore us and you mustn't let other people run me down. I live in the ancestral mansion of all our forbears, and I'm the oldest; so it doesn't matter where the old lady falls ill, but if she were to be laid out somewhere else my name would be mud. Help me, brothers, to call a carriage at once to take her home. You and your wives can stay with us if you like."

Second Brother sat there calmly combing his moustache. "How open and above board you sound!" he chortled. "But it's no use. You can't fool me. The truth is, like it or lump it, it's a stroke of luck for me, her falling ill here. I'm not letting you carry her off."

When Third Brother also put in his claim, their sister warned, "Don't let the neighbours hear you. Want them to laugh? Do you know what I think?"

"Just tell us, sister."

"You want what mother has round her waist, don't you?"

"Oh no!"

"No? I can tell you all she has there is part of my dowry."

True, that pewter had gone with her when she got married.

"When the old lady insisted on taking it away, how could I stop her? So I let her carry it off. But do stop fighting over her; she's too old to stand it. Let her nurse her illness here. Second Brother can find an empty chest, which we can inspect to make sure there's nothing wrong with it. Then we'll take off this pouch round the old lady's waist and lock it in the chest — I'll keep the key. To be on the safe side you three can seal up the chest. If the old lady recovers, we'll let her fasten on her pouch again. If she passes away, I'll tell you what to do with this little legacy. Strictly speaking a daughter should have the same share as the sons, but I don't want a cent of her property; so I'll take charge. I'll give the old lady's legacy to whoever's treated her best; not a cent will go to anyone who's been unfilial."

The three brothers held up their thumbs. "Right, right! We're not up to you! That's the way to do it."

A chest was found and examined. The daughter undressed her mother, and the brothers removed the pouch by clipping and cutting its cords without seeing what was inside. They dumped it, clanking, into the chest, closed the lid, locked it and pasted on three seals. After that they went to attend to the old lady.

Then what happened? Forty days later, when medicine proved of no avail, the old lady died. Then how filial First Master was! He bought her a hardwood coffin inlaid with gold, over five inches thick, spread with gold and covered with silver, with seven big gold coins below her and seven huge pearls. He had to raise the money for this by selling his house. Wasn't that dutiful? Second Master couldn't buy another coffin, but he set up a great funeral awning in his house with archways stretching across the street, a bell tower, a drum tower, a big bright mirror at the gate, and an imposing inscription. There Buddhists, Taoists, lamas and nuns said masses for forty-nine days. Second Master soon spent all his money and had to sell his house too. What about Third Master? He sold his house and ran into debt to hire three shifts of sixty-four bier-bearers. This cortège covered half the street, burning golden and silver paper mountains all the way. So he showed *his* piety by giving his ma this fine send-off!

Would an unfilial son have sold his house to buy his mother a coffin? To have masses said for her? To provide a cortège? Oh, they were filial all right, yet in a peculiar way — though the funeral was so sumptuous, no one wept! Apart from wailing a couple of times when paper money was burnt to the old lady, none of the family wept. The neighbours were puzzled by this strange behaviour. The grandchildren might not have the sense to cry, the daughters-in-law came from different families and might not be too fond of their mother-in-law, but why didn't her own sons weep? Not a tear did they shed! Not only that, though in deep mourning they laughed and chatted as usual, just letting their moustaches grow a little. They strutted about, even humming tunes from a lively opera. One neighbour asked in surprise:

"Second Master, did you put up this canopy to make a fine show?"

A fine show! Second Master liked the sound of that. He laughed. "No, to atone for our sins, not to make a show."

"They say you're not too well off, had to sell your house to have masses said for your mother — that's truly filial!"

"It was no more than my duty. What is a house anyway? Only a poor specimen of a man lives on his inheritance — better spend it on the old lady."

"How filial! Mind if I ask a blunt question?"

"What is it?"

"Why don't you weep?"

Second Master pulled a long face. "What a question to ask! Why weep? Death comes to us all, doesn't it? Mama was seventy-four this year, she lived to a great old age. So why weep? If I wept myself to death would that bring her back to life? She had a happy death. We must all die sooner or later."

"What makes you so pleased?"

"Why shouldn't I be pleased? She had a happy death. If it weren't against the rules, we'd be staging operas. This is no way for you to talk, you have parents too and should bury them this way."

The brothers fobbed off all the neighbours with this talk of a happy death, and they and their wives shed not a tear when the cortège set out and the coffin was interred.

After the burial the three brothers and their wives took off their mourning in the graveyard. "Sister, sister," they urged, "come back with us by carriage."

But their sister knew what to do. Sitting in the graveyard she asked, "Go back with you? No, I must go home, I've been away for months!"

"No hurry, come back with us first to clear up some business, then you can go home and rest. In a couple of days we'll all come over to thank you."

"No need for that. You're thinking about that chest.

eh? Go back first to see if the seals have been tampered with."

"We looked before we came out — no one's touched them."

"I'm not responsible then! Suppose I give you the key. Remember what I told you. By rights a daughter should have her share, but I don't want it. Instead I have the right to decide which of you deserves this legacy. It looks as if all three of you were filial, selling your houses and running into debt to give mother a good funeral. So you should divide it into three equal shares. Count me out, I don't want a cent. The seals haven't been touched, have they? So I'm not responsible. I'll give you the key — don't start squabbling over your shares!"

"That's right. Good for you, sister. We'll be coming to thank you."

The three brothers went home almost beside themselves. When their wives had joined them they inspected the chest. No, the seals had not been touched.

They tore off the seals, opened the chest, and lugged the pouch on to the *kang*. Their wives cut open the pouch with knives and scissors, then poured the contents out, clinking! At the sight First Master ground his teeth. "Dammit, there's no gold, and this bit of silver doesn't amount to much. . . . In any case, *is* this silver?"

Third Master said, "Try biting it. Silver won't dent."

The brothers and their wives each bit a piece. They found their teeth left marks!

"Pewter, that's what it is! Heavens, what a dirty trick! Who put ma up to this? She's done for us!"

They all burst into tears.

"I'm not responsible then!... I'll give you the key — don't start squabbling over your shares!"

That puzzled the neighbours. They said, "What's wrong with this family? They didn't cry over the old lady's death or burial. Now when the funeral's over they can't stop crying. Let's reason with them."

They came over to remonstrate.

"Done for! It's no use your talking, we're ruined. Now ma's dead, how are we to live?"

"Wasn't it a happy death?"

"Happy death — we'll never be able to pay for it!"

(Told by Zhang Shouchen)

Returning by Boat in the Rain

IN the old society the rich had pots of money. It was very easy for them to make money. Why? Because money breeds money. And it was a case of easy come easy go. There's an anecdote about this which may amuse you.

In the time of the Republic there lived in the west city in Beijing a rich man known as Second Master Hua. His real name was Hua Yuanquan, but he was called Wastrel Hua. How was it that the poor couldn't get a share of all his pots of money? When beggars called at his house he went out, getting into his car at the gate or in the courtyard. How did he spend his money? In the third year of the Republic, 1914, he spent twenty thousand dollars on four caged grasshoppers. Because he threw his money around like that they called him Wastrel Hua. Yet not a cent could the poor get unless they swindled him.

Then a well-known swindler in Beijing, nicknamed the Mastermind, thought of a way to swindle Wastrel Hua out of fifty thousand dollars. How did he go about it? He rented a grand mansion in the east city. All the antiques and furniture in it were rented; all the cooks, maidservants, slave girls, concubines and young mistresses were hired — all in the plot. The Mastermind got some acquaintances to introduce him to Wastrel Hua, inviting him one day to a feast, the next day to an opera, until the two of them were on friendly terms.

One day it rained. Wastrel Hua was sitting at home when the Mastermind arrived in a car — a rented car — to take him to his mansion for a meal. "It's a wet day, Second Master. Come and take pot-luck with me." Wastrel Hua agreed, and off they went together.

The Mastermind's mansion was full of antiques, fine furniture and old paintings. Wastrel Hua thought: Why, he's richer than I am and lives in better style! Little did he know that everything was rented. In the course of conversation the Mastermind said:

"Second Master Hua, my forbears collected antiques, good furnishings and old paintings. I hear that's your taste too. So I'd like your opinion of an old painting that's come down to me. Will you condescend to look at it?"

"A family heirloom, fine! You are doing me too much honour."

The Mastermind brought out a scroll. "Here it is." He unrolled this painting entitled *Returning by Boat in the Rain*. In the background were hills, in the foreground a boat on the river, and there was a bridge with a boy on it in the middle. It was very windy and pouring with rain so that he was having a hard time crossing the bridge. The picture was well-painted but undated, and the name of the artist on it was not well-known.

Just at this point a maid came in to announce, "The meal's ready, master."

"All right, serve it."

The Mastermind rolled up the scroll and put it on a shelf. A square table was brought in and they sat down to eat. Cooks, maids and slave girls came and went waiting on them, and the meal lasted for a good two hours.

By the time they had finished and the table had been cleared away, the rain outside had stopped.

The Mastermind asked, "Second Master, what did you think of that painting?"

"I couldn't tell when it was painted."

"Have another look." He unrolled the scroll again.

Wastrel Hua commented, "Although there's no date, the paper looks old." The signature He Minsan was not the name of any famous artist. "Who was He Minsan?" he asked. Then looking at the bridge he exclaimed in surprise, "Whatever's happened! Just now the boy was holding an unfurled umbrella, but now he has a furled one. How come?"

"That's why this is an heirloom, Second Master. Yes, just now the umbrella was unfurled as it was raining. We treasure this painting because in wet weather the umbrella is unfurled, when the rain stops it is furled."

Could such a thing be?

"Why, this is a real treasure!" exclaimed Wastrel Hua. Being such a collector of antiques and old paintings, he longed to acquire this scroll but didn't like to make an offer himself. Back home he asked some friends to purchase it for him. When the Mastermind refused to sell, he sent people to feast him and negotiate with him, till finally a price was named — a hundred thousand dollars. Even Wastrel Hua thought a hundred thousand too much, and made his friends bargain with the Mastermind till he brought the figure down to fifty thousand. And so the painting changed hands.

The painting was brought to Wastrel Hua on a fine

day, so of course the umbrella was furled. In great glee he rolled it up and put it away, then lost no time in inviting his friends to a meal to admire his new purchase. But strange to say no date was fixed on the invitation cards, which simply specified "the next rainy day". Why was that? He wanted to show them this painting when it rained.

One day it poured with rain, and all his friends came.

"Friends," said Wastrel Hua, "I have a painting here which was someone's family heirloom; but much as he valued it I prevailed upon him to sell it. I want you all to see it. It's raining outside, isn't it? When I brought it home, the boy on the bridge was holding a furled umbrella; but whenever it rains that boy unfurls his umbrella, not furling it again until the rain stops."

His guests crowded round eagerly to look. But when Wastrel Hua unrolled the scroll he was flummoxed: Why was the umbrella still furled? What was wrong?

His guests asked, "Didn't you say, sir, that he unfurls the umbrella when it rains?"

Red in the face he stammered, "Y-yes ... the rain can't be heavy enough yet. Let's roll it up now and have another look later."

Before long the rain outside was coming down in buckets. His guests asked to see the painting again, but still the umbrella was furled. Presently the rain stopped and, taking another look, they saw it was still furled. Not liking to make any comment, when the meal was over they left. Wastrel Hua was furious! All right, he's swindled me, I must have it out with him! He went straight to the east city.

Wouldn't you have expected the Mastermind to clear

"The set of two scrolls, one with the umbrella unfurled, one with it furled. In wet weather you look at this painting, on fine days at that."

out? But no, he stayed put. Why? To provoke Wastrel Hua.

Wastrel Hua complained to him, "Call yourself my friend? Why swindle me and sting me fifty thousand for that painting! Why cheat me like that?"

"How can you accuse me of cheating you, Second Master?"

"Didn't you say the umbrella in that painting is unfurled when it rains, furled when it's fine? It was furled when I bought it, but why did it stay furled in pouring rain? You cheated me!"

The Mastermind chortled, "No, I didn't cheat you. I asked you for a hundred thousand, but you'd only give fifty thousand, right?"

"So what? Won't the magic work for fifty thousand less?"

"It's not that. You don't understand. I asked for a hundred thousand for the set — you should have bought the set."

"What set?"

"The set of two scrolls, one with the umbrella unfurled, one with it furled. In wet weather you look at this painting, on fine days at that."

(Told by Liu Baorui)

Borrowing a Light

THIS *xiangsheng* I'm going to tell you is called *There Are No Ghosts.* You believe in ghosts, but have you seen any? No. In the old days people sacrificed to the Kitchen God on the twenty-third of the twelfth lunar month, buying sweetmeats for him and putting up the couplet:

Go up to heaven to speak well of us,

And bring good fortune back.

Why buy sweetmeats? So that, after accepting their offerings, the god wouldn't speak badly of them to the Jade Emperor. Some smeared sugar on his mouth as well, to stick his lips together. But that was a silly thing to do: he couldn't say bad things, couldn't say good things either. Why not? His lips were sealed!

If there are no ghosts, why were people afraid of them? Because of the stories they were told as children about fearful-looking ghosts with red hair, green eyeballs and fangs. These were based in fact on idols carved in wood or moulded in clay. Certain superstitious folk also believed that some men had "real fire" on their heads and a lamp on each shoulder. Walking in a dark alley, if such a man was afraid he would cough, then thwack his head — Whack! Whack! Whack! Why do that? His head wasn't making any trouble, so why thwack it? To strike fire from it to frighten ghosts away. What rubbish! How can you strike a light from your head? If you could, so much the better; you wouldn't have to buy matches to light your cigarettes. "Want a light for your cigarette, brother?" (Whacks his head.) There, it's lit up! Can such things happen?

Once there was a timid fellow, so scared of ghosts that he couldn't walk naturally. Why not? For fear his head would fail to light up, the lamps on his shoulders would fall off, and a ghost would throttle him. So he shuffled along with head, shoulders and body rigid. (Walks like a zombie.) Who in his senses walks that way? He had just reached the middle of an alley when someone behind took fright at the sight of him. He wondered: Is that a man or a ghost? A ghost? Didn't look like one. A man? No man walked that way. He decided: Never mind whether it's a man or a ghost, I'll follow it and when it stops I'll stop too. If it turns round I'll throw a brick at it. So the fellow behind followed slowly.

The man in front heard him. Help! Here's a ghost come to catch me. He decided to have a look. If it was a man he'd have company, wouldn't he? But if he turned round too quickly the lamps on his shoulders might go out and the ghost might throttle him. So he rotated slowly and stiffly around, and the man behind fled like this, crying, "Help! It's a ghost!" He threw his brick, wham! It landed bang in the middle of the first man's forehead, so that he stopped shuffling along and took to his heels. Back home he had just rubbed on ointment and bandaged up his head when his son came in.

"A fearful thing just happened, dad," said his son. "I saw a zombie. I chucked a brick at him. You. . . ."

"Oh, so it was you who threw it?!"

But it was his own fault for shuffling along like that.

Another time too there was a misunderstanding. A man hung himself on a gnarled tree on the river bank outside town. Why did he do that? That was really a black, man-eating, spooky world before Liberation. This poor fellow had been forced to borrow money, and the interest piled up so fast that he couldn't pay it. The money-lender came one day to dun him.

"Are you trying to back out, you pauper? Even if you die, your ghost will have to pay up!"

The poor man had no way out, so he hung himself by the river. As it was growing dark, the authorities decided not to cut him down for a post-mortem till the next day; but meantime his corpse must not be moved, Wang San the watchman must keep an eye on it. Wang San thought: I must find a way to stop passers-by from bumping into it. So from a nearby grocery he got a stick of incense which he lit, then put in the corpse's hand. That should do the trick he imagined. When people saw the light they'd steer clear of it. He bought himself some liquor and sat down on the steps of a big gateway opposite, hugging the jug of liquor and muttering, "I say, mate, we always hit it off so well, why didn't you turn to your poor brothers for help? Now you've made us all feel bad, so I'm drinking to drown my grief." He took a swig. "Have some grog? No, you won't drink?" He took another swig. When Wang San had downed all the liquor he dozed off.

Then along came a man who wanted to smoke but had forgotten his matches. When he reached the gnarled tree on the river bank and saw the burning incense, he decided to ask for a light. You know the rule in such cases. If I want to borrow a light from someone, I don't look at him till I've lit my cigarette. Then I offer him one. "Like a smoke?" Isn't that how it is? Well, that's what this fellow did. He didn't look up at first, just made a bee-line for that light, though he couldn't think why anyone should stand there at midnight holding an incense-stick. "Excuse me, can I borrow your light? (Goes through the motions of lighting a cigarette, then looks up.) Like one of mine? . . . (A shocked silence. . . .) Oh?! It's you!"

When he saw the man hanging there, his head reeled, his hair stood on end, he was petrified. Why? Because the dead man was his debtor. He thought: Heavens! I really hounded him to death, so now he'll get even with me! He flung away his cigarette, still clutching the stick of incense, and too terrified to run stumped slowly forward. Just then Wang San the watchman opened his blurry eyes and saw the lighted incense-stick jerking forward. He thought: Hey! Are you leaving? No can do! The corpse mustn't be moved an inch, I'll have to fetch you back. Wang San scurried after him, and his thudding steps scared the money-lender still more. He thought: Mother! He's come down! Imagining that the dead man was chasing him, his legs nearly gave way. Wang San overtook him and grabbed

He ... couldn't think why anyone should stand there at midnight holding an incense-stick. "Excuse me, can I borrow your light? ... Oh? I ..."

his neck from behind. Then, with a yell of terror, the money-lender dropped dead. Wang San lugged him back by the legs and hoisted him up to the tree. (Goes through the motions.) "Wherever you run to, mate, I'll have to lug you back. You're not to move an inch till tomorrow's post-mortem! Let me hang you up again. (Goes through the motions.) Hey! What's this other one doing here?!"

(Told by Guo Quanbao)

Stropping a Razor

EACH trade has its special tricks and its special patter. Sometimes you can tell a man's line the moment he opens his mouth. In the old society a man's profession could be seen too from his clothes. See this fellow in a long gown, short outer waistcoat and hexagonal brocade cap? He's a travelling merchant for sure. A long gown, mandarin jacket and gauze cap mark the manager of a big restaurant. Most labourers wear short jackets and dress simply. This man in a western suit, his leather shoes so polished that you can see your face in them, must be the director of some firm or a bank manager. That one in a western suit, with a queue, greasy boots and a cane — he's like nobody on earth.

You don't always have to size up a man's clothes or hear him speak to know his profession. How do you know? Watch his movements when he sits down. How do fiddlers keep their hands in? They hold a small bow with a string two inches long, and practise fingering it wherever they are. If they go out in a hurry and forget it, no matter where they sit their thumbs and first fingers keep vibrating like this. (Demonstrates.) Anyone can tell at a glance that they are fiddlers. And look at this way of sitting (demonstrates) with three fingers flicking back and forth; that's an accountant flicking the beads of his abacus. This one with all five fingers moving right and left (demonstrates) is a pianist. And this gentleman sitting like this (demonstrates), with not only his fingers but his whole wrist trembling, it goes without saying is a paralytic!

How did barbers keep in training in the old days? They shaved the back of a comb or practised with a chopstick. One might sit there moving his wrist like this (demonstrates), three of his fingers crooked from force of habit. Why keep on training like that? When business was slack a barber could get by; when it was brisk he had to shave ten heads without stopping to rest, and if his wrist ached or his fingers slipped he might gash the customer and make him mad.

When I was young we lived next door to a barber, and I often called on him. One day two of the barbers made me laugh. How come? One of them was skilled, the other green. The skilled barber looked down on the greenhorn. He jeered, "Take it from me, Number Three, you can scrape by here, but anywhere else you wouldn't earn your keep."

"Don't you look down on me, Number Two. I can always go home to farm, which is more than you could! Barbering is all you're fit for, so don't run down other people."

"Well, you're not up to me. Let me show you." He stropped the razor twice on the palm of his hand which was calloused from sharpening his razor. If the blade was blunt, that was the quickest, easiest way to whet it. After stropping it he turned the razor over.

"Can you do that?"

"Easy. Just wait till I've finished this shave."

Number Three was shaving a customer, and now he saw that he'd shaved off one of his eyebrows. The customer was dozing. He woke him to ask:

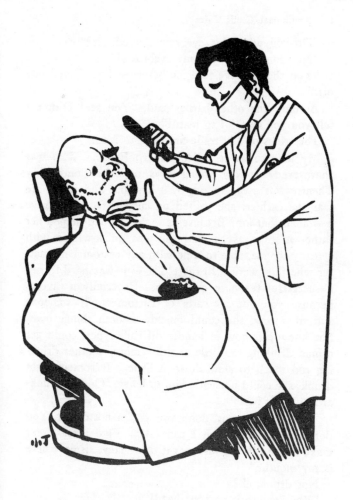

"Do you want this eyebrow shaved, sir?"
"No, don't you touch my eyebrows!"
"You should have told me before — I've shaved one off."

"Do you want this eyebrow shaved, sir?"

"No, don't you touch my eyebrows!"

"You should have told me before — I've shaved one off."

At once the other barber said, "You see! Didn't I tell you you've a lot to learn!"

The tricks of any trade are hard to learn.

My joke today is called "Sharp Eyes". Who was sharp-eyed? In my young days opposite South City Theatre was a tavern run by a husband and wife. He was the cashier, she waited on customers. Why give a woman that job? Because as a girl she had helped her father in this tavern, and she was quick-witted with a ready tongue, able to cope with any customer no matter who they were. In the old days it was hard to run a successful teahouse or tavern. Especially a tavern, because you got all sorts of customers. If someone started a row, she could quickly smooth things over. She knew just how to handle difficult types, could get a man drinking too little to drink more, another drinking too much to slow down a little. If someone got drunk, she could persuade him to leave. Once a drunkard raved at her:

"I tell you, missus, don't worry, I'm not drunk. You don't know how much I can take. Five litres won't make me drunk. I just toss it off. Hey, sister, where is my mouth?"

Not drunk, eh?

"Your mouth is on your head!"

Splash! He emptied a bowl of liquor on his head. "I tell you, missus, just ask around, most everyone in the whole of north China knows me. If this little tavern of yours is short of anything, just let me know.

You can send the department store over to my place. . . ."

"Fine! You'd better go back now, I'll send it presently."

"Right, I'm off."

Not only was that woman a good talker, she was very observant too. She had only to exchange a few remarks with any customer to know what trade he was in. Sometimes she could tell simply from his clothes. Or, failing that, from his movements. Regular customers, knowing this, gave her the nickname Sharp Eyes.

One day my neighbour Second Li said to me, "I'll treat you to a drink." I told him I was no drinker. "We'll go to have some fun then. I often drink in that South City tavern with the manageress nicknamed Sharp Eyes. After a few words with any customer, if she can't tell what his job is she stands treat. I told her I'd take a friend there tomorrow, and I bet she wouldn't be able to see what his job was. The way you dress and the serious way you talk are more like a shopkeeper than a *xiangsheng* performer; so I'm sure she won't be able to guess what you do. Be careful, though, how you talk there tomorrow.

"All right," I agreed.

The next day I went with him. At South City Archway I bought a pair of shoes and took them with me to the tavern. I saw it consisted of three rooms, all spick and span.

"So you're back, Mr Li. Do sit down."

"Sister, everyone says you're smart. Can you tell who this friend is I've brought along today?"

"Please sit down, gentlemen."

Li and I took seats, and she brought us two pots of liquor and four side-dishes. "What's your friend's honourable name, Mr Li?"

I put in, "Just call me whatever you like."

"Oh, what an idea!"

"My name is Guo."

"What have you got there, Mr Guo?"

"Shoes!"

"Where did you buy them?"

"In a shoe shop."

"Ha! How do you find our liquor?"

"Not bad, tastes fiery."

"Oh, you must be a *xiangsheng* performer."

"Why, how did you know, sister?"

"From the amusing way you talk. I wanted to laugh just now, but didn't like to. You said I could call you any name I liked, said your shoes were bought in a shoe shop. Well, of course, you don't buy shoes from a pastry shop! Are you a *xiangsheng* artist?"

I admitted, "Yes, I am."

After finishing our drinks Li and I left. On the way back he scolded, "I told you to be careful how you talked, but you had to crack jokes till she knew you were a *xiangsheng* performer."

I realized then how quick on the uptake she was. "Never mind, tomorrow I'll introduce two of my friends, and I'm sure she won't be able to see what they do."

I had in mind Wu Xibiao from the barber's shop next door, and Zhang Dekui who plays martial roles in Beijing opera. When they came the next day I said, "Let me introduce Mr Wu and Mr Zhang. This is Second Brother Li. How would you size them up?"

Li looked at Zhang and said, "No go, Rongqi. Even

I can see at a glance that Mr Zhang is an actor. Look at his prominent eyes, his bulging forehead and the way he throws out his chest as if he were Wu Song going to catch a tiger!"

I saw he was right and objected to Zhang, "Must you keep striking a pose?"

He said, "Suppose I cover up by stooping a little and half closing my eyes, eh?"

"Well, just be careful there. What do you make of Mr Wu, Second Brother?"

Wu Xibiao was young and natty. In his western suit and spectacles he looked like a scholar or a bank manager. "What would you say he does, Brother Li?"

"Can't tell."

"He's a barber."

Li stared at him. "Well, he doesn't look like one, looks more like a comprador."

Wu boasted, "I tell you, Mr Li, no one can ever guess that I'm a barber."

I thought, confound it! You may look like a scholar, but the moment you open your mouth you give the show away. So I said, "Can't you change your accent? After all these years in Tianjin can't you speak with a Tianjin accent?"

So he switched over.

"Don't mix that with your local dialect," I warned him.

"I won't mix them," he promised.

Second Brother Li was very pleased.

The next day Li took the three of us to the tavern and ushered us in.

"Please sit down," he said. "Sister, everyone knows how smart you are. Yesterday you saw that my young friend here was a *xiangsheng* performer. Can you tell what these two do?"

"Oh, what are your friends' honourable names?"

"This is Zhang, that's Wu."

"Do have a seat, Mr Zhang!"

"Thank you."

"What would you like to drink, sir?"

"I'm not much of a drinker, anything will do. It's all the same to me, with some cold and hot dishes."

The manageress saw that he had staring eyes and a prominent forehead, but he talked in a high voice like a girl. "How do you find this liquor? To your taste?"

"This liquor? Let me taste it. (Declaims in operatic style) This liquor, ha...."

I gave a start and hastily put in, "Try some of the dishes!" He had nearly let the cat out of the bag.

The manageress came and went, keeping her eye on both men without being able to guess their occupations. But time always tells. After drinking for a while Mr Zhang went out to buy some cigarettes. When he came back he gave the show away. How? He came in as another customer went out. As the door was narrow, he turned sidewise, then took a pace forward and threw back his shoulders as he came to a halt. (Demonstrates.)

The manageress exclaimed, "Why, Mr Zhang, you're an actor."

"How do you know, sister?"

"The way you made a stage entrance, as if drums and gongs were going *qiang-qiang, beng-deng, qiang!* Aren't you an actor?"

"Yes, no use pretending I'm not. Well, it's up to you, Mr Wu."

"Never mind, sit down! Let's the two of us play the finger-guessing game."

When the manageress came over to fill their cups, Wu gave himself away too.

"You're a good drinker, Mr Wu. Will you have a drink with me?"

As he took the cup, that did it. "Thank you, sister." (Demonstrates.)

People accepting a wine cup take it in one hand and raise the other in salute. "Thank you, thank you." But not Wu. He took the cup in his right hand, holding it like this, as if holding a razor.

Then Sharp Eyes asked, "Mr Wu, aren't you a barber?"

"Ha! How did you guess that, sister?" (Involuntarily slaps the palm of his hand.)

"Isn't that where you strop the razor?"

"Still stropping it, am I?!" (Demonstrates.)

(Told by Guo Rongqi)

[32]

单口相声故事选

张寿臣等

熊猫丛书

＊

中国文学出版社出版

（中国北京百万庄路24号）

中国国际图书贸易总公司发行

（中国北京车公庄西路21号）

北京邮政信箱第399号　　邮政编码100044

外文印刷厂印刷

1983年（36开）第1版

1990年第二次印刷

I S B N　7－5071－0063－4／Ⅰ·57

00400

10－E－1756P